DATE DUE			

COPING

WITH

Cliques

COPING WITH

Cliques

Lee A. Peck

THE ROSEN PUBLISHING GROUP, INC./NEW YORK

Published in 1992 by The Rosen Publishing Group, Inc.
29 East 21st Street, New York, NY 10010

First Edition

51890

Library of Congress Cataloging-in-Publication Data

92-18547

Peck, Lee A.
    Coping with cliques/ Lee A. Peck. -- 1st ed.
        117p.   cm.
    Includes bibliographical references and index.
    Summary: Discusses some of the positive and negative aspects
of cliques and offers suggestions for dealing with various situations
involving friends.
    ISBN 0-8239-1412-7
    1. Peer pressure in adolescence--United States--Juvenile
literature. 2. Social groups--Juvenile literature. 3. Adolescent
psychology--United States--Juvenile literature.   [1. Social groups.
2. Peer pressure. 3. Interpersonal relations. 4. Friendship.] I. Title.
II. Title: Cliques.
HQ799.2.P44P43   1992
303.3'27--dc20

                                                    92-12380
                                                         CIP
                                                          AC

Manufactured in the United States of America

*To my son, Davis, who
is a seventh-grader
and just learning
to cope
with cliques.*

ABOUT THE AUTHOR ◇

L ee A. Peck is a journalist and a college teacher in Fort Collins, Colorado.

Peck holds a bachelor's degree in technical journalism and a master's degree in communication development, both from Colorado State University, Fort Collins. Her graduate work emphasized nonfiction writing and adolescent literature. She has spent time as a volunteer with a variety of teen writing projects.

She lives in Fort Collins with her husband and son.

Acknowledgments

Thanks go to the junior high and high school counselors of the Fort Collins, Colorado, Poudre R-1 School District for sharing their knowledge about teenagers. Also thanks to Jep Enck, president of the Human Resource Institute and a former junior high teacher and youth center director; he provided many helpful tips given here.

For telling me of their personal experiences in coping with cliques, thanks go to many of my former students at the University of Northern Colorado, Greeley, and at Front Range Community College, Fort Collins.

Thanks also for her contributions to Mary Ann Clemons of Fort Collins, who has a master's degree in psychiatric nursing and many years of experience in helping adolescents.

Contents

Introduction: Fitting in Where You Belong

• From kindergarten to sixth grade, Jason attended the same school. He liked going there because he was comfortable; many of his classmates lived in his neighborhood and were part of his "group." The number of children in each class was small too—no more than twenty or twenty-five.

Now, however, Jason has started junior high; young people from several grade schools all go to one school—and the classes seem huge. Some have as many as thirty-five students. Jason never sees his neighborhood buddies until after school, and they are beginning to make new friends and to ignore him.

Suddenly Jason is shy; he misses the comfortable life-style and group of friends he had in grade school. How can he cope?

• Sara is in a similar situation to Jason's; however, she is making the transition from junior high to high school. Though Sara still hangs around with her group from junior high, she feels she needs to move on and make new friends.

She's uncomfortable that some of her old friends

don't care about their grades and some want to try drinking alcohol. She wants new experiences—but not that kind.

But Sara is afraid to leave her clique; she's afraid she won't be accepted into another one. She'd love to make friends with the students who work on the school newspaper because she loves to write. So how does Sarah leave her old friends and make new ones? How does she change groups?

- Matt, a junior in high school, has just moved from his hometown to a city 300 miles away. His family had to move because of his father's work. At his old school, Matt was very popular and was part of an "in" group.

   In his new high Matt feels really confused. His friends in his old group were always there; he was never alone. His clique was supportive, yet he could not dress the way he wanted to or date some of the girls he wanted to—the group always had to approve. Should he seek out a group again? Or would it be better to find just a few close friends who wouldn't care how he dressed or whom he dated? Did he need a clique to survive high school?

   Unfortunately, Matt also feels angry with his parents for making him *have* to make this decision in the first place. He's angry that they have so much control over his life: Why did they have to move, anyway?

   What can he do to make the best of this situation?

- Finally, Melissa has just moved too. She has moved from her hometown and high school to a college 500 miles away in another state.

Melissa was pegged a nerd in grade school, and she never outgrew that label all the way through senior year; most of her classmates ignored her. Now Melissa has a chance for a fresh start: No one at college has heard her called a nerd. No one at college knows her reputation.

If Melissa can just build up her self-confidence and self-esteem, she has a chance of making more friends than she has ever had. What are some helpful hints for her to follow while she makes the transition?

The above stories are composites of young people who were interviewed about their relationships and involvements with social cliques. All of them have one thing in common: They were trying to cope with friendships—new and old.

As young people move from grade school through high school, from high school to college, or from one city to another, they experience many life changes.

With these changes, friendships take different turns. Sometimes young people move on and make new friends, yet others want to cling to cliques that seem safe and familiar.

There is no doubt that friends can be an important part of a young person's life. A clique can be a kind of support group made up of people with similar interests.

Sometimes, however, young people in cliques stop making decisions for themselves: They end up conforming to what a group wants them to be. They are not doing things that they really want to do, and thus they are losing their individuality.

Thus, being part of an "in" group does not always mean happiness. For instance, because of pressure from the clique young people may find themselves participating in activities, such as drinking or doing drugs, that they would rather avoid.

Friendships, however, all come down to what a young person really wants. Teens need to learn to choose friends they are comfortable with.

There are many ways to cope with cliques and friendships, and this book was written to offer suggestions on how to handle a variety of situations. Advice is offered on how to survive a move, how to make the transition from one school level to the next, how to meet new friends and keep the old ones, and how to end unhealthy relationships.

Most important, self-image and self-confidence are addressed. Suggestions are offered on how to avoid trying to be more than you are, how to just "be yourself." Does a person really have to lose his or her individuality just because of joining a group?

CHAPTER 1

Your Self-Image

f you have high self-esteem, you feel confident and believe in yourself. You can accept constructive criticism, and you do not feel threatened by failure.

In other words, you don't put yourself down; you are able to deal with whatever obstacles you meet when it comes to cliques and friendships.

Risk-Taking and Self-Esteem

High self-esteem involves risk-taking, so allow yourself the right to be wrong. No one can be perfect.

If you join the wrong school organization, allow yourself the right to get out and find something different to occupy your time with. If you're with the wrong group of friends, admit it. Seek out new friendships.

Think of Thomas Edison and his invention of the light bulb: He tried more than forty times before he got it right.

Edison didn't give up. He kept taking risks.

To evaluate your self-esteem, you need to evaluate who you are.

Junior high and high school counselors suggest the following questions to help you with your evaluation:

- Do you feel confident about who you are?
- Do you find it easy to make friends?
- Are you ever pressured by your peers to do something you don't want to do?
- Do you make fun of other people? Do you judge them by how they look?

Losing It

Bruce Bower in a *Science News* article, "Teenage Turning Point," writes that young people may experience a decline in self-esteem as they enter their adolescent years, "a time marked by the abrupt move from the relatively cloistered confines of elementary school to the more complex social and academic demands of junior high school."

A 1991 report by the American Association of University Women shows that girls often experience declines in self-esteem that far outpace those reported by boys. For both sexes, however, the sharpest decline occurs at the beginning of junior high.

Jim

Jim, a seventh-grader, failed to make the basketball team. It was his first year of junior high school, and he had practiced the game all summer and fall.

When he didn't make the team, he was so embarrassed that he didn't want to face the world. He shut himself off from his friends and family. He stayed home sick from school as often as he could and refused to participate in any outside activities; he especially avoided school basketball games.

His friends missed his company, though; a couple of them did not make the team either, but they decided to try again next year. They wanted Jim to practice with them, but he refused.

Coping through High Self-Esteem

Jim suddenly had very low self-esteem; he was becoming a loner who expected to fail again in the future.

He would rather isolate himself than take part in activities such as basketball practice.

Jim was very sensitive to ridicule. He didn't realize that nobody in his group was going to ridicule him— several were in the same position he was in.

To survive in the world of junior high and high school, you need all the self-esteem you can get.

Self-esteem will help you to cope better with problems you may face, and it will also help you resist peer pressure.

Learn to like yourself and not worry about what others think. Realize what you are, not what you are not.

Building Your Self-Esteem

Jep Enck of the Human Resource Institute suggests "putting the steam in your self-esteem" by considering the following points:

1. **Focus on your positives.**
   It's easy to forget that you are a special person. Take some time to write a list of the attributes you are proud of such as intelligence, humor,

athletic ability, and so on. Be specific, and keep the list handy for additions or to read when you are feeling down.

2. **Look in the mirror.**
   Take a reflective moment to see yourself as others do. Are you taking care of your body? Are you eating well? Exercising? Practicing good grooming? How you look is a reflection of how you feel about yourself.

3. **Associate with winners.**
   Choosing the right friends and associates will help you to surround yourself with positive energy, enthusiasm, and a "can do" attitude. Be careful not to compare yourself to others; be okay with who you are.

4. **Manage your first impressions.**
   Many studies in human communications emphasize the importance of first impressions. Look people in the eye, reach out with a handshake, and volunteer your name first. Try to use the person's name often in conversation. Eye contact is vital in informing people how you feel about yourself, and it conveys sincerity.

5. **Acknowledge those around you.**
   Take time to notice the little positives in others. Don't be stingy with compliments and congratulations. By putting positive energy out to others, you are bound to receive some back. Say thank you when you are the receiver of praise.

6. **Choose your words carefully.**
   Everything you say about yourself and about others is carved into your memory. Negative self-talk and put-downs of others have a way of influencing the way you look at life.

7. **Commit yourself to growth.**

Know that you are special now but that with each new day you can improve. Being open to new thoughts, experiences, and feelings helps you to grow. Don't hesitate to ask questions and admit ignorance. Accept honest criticism from caring people; it will help you learn more about yourself.

8. **Laugh often.**

People who are quick to laugh and smile tend to like themselves and enjoy the company of many types of people. Your ability to find humor in everyday life will help you get through the tough times and give you perspective in working out your problems.

Humans Make Mistakes

Remember that failure is not permanent; failure means learning, and it will make you a stronger person. In other words, Enck says, think to yourself: "I'm brilliant because I screwed up a lot."

Appreciate the qualities you have now.

When it comes to friends, if you're not in the "in" clique it's okay.

Remember, you are a good, worthwhile person. Quiet self-acceptance will clue others into the fact that you are a good person to know.

Jim Wakes Up

Jim stayed inside and away from his friends all winter. When spring came and the snow melted, he found himself out in the driveway with his basketball. He couldn't help it; the beautiful weather drew him outside.

Two of his friends happened to walk by, and they began to shoot baskets with him. When they were worn out, the three of them sat down and talked.

Jim's friends told him they were glad to see him outside and playing basketball; they asked if they could come by the next day. Jim agreed. He had finally accepted that he had failed and that it wasn't the end of the world. He was ready to try again.

But he had also decided that even if he didn't make the team the next year, he wouldn't give up; he enjoyed basketball too much.

Talk It Out

Jim was finally able to pull himself out of his depression and period of low self-esteem—all it took was time and beautiful spring weather. Others may find it hard to find self-esteem on their own, however.

Talk to an adult who is close to you if you are having a hard time coping.

Consider talking with your parents. They may suggest that you see a therapist of some kind to help you cope through a particularly difficult time. (Seeking outside help is discussed in Chapter 15.)

In any situation, don't stop talking to people. Find someone to listen to you.

CHAPTER 2

The Road from Grade School to High School

The transitions from grade school to junior high to high school are big ones, and these steps to larger schools can be scary. What is there to look forward to? Strange places and strange faces.

Young people can feel as if they are going from being top banana at one school to the lowest step on the social ladder at the next.

When it comes to friends and cliques, a question that young people may ask themselves is, "Where do I belong now?"

Adolescents are looking for identity. As their identification switches from their family to their friends, they may look at cliques they would like to be part of—or stop being part of.

Through their junior high and high school years, adolescents look for teens—just like themselves—who want to try out new ideas and discuss new thoughts.

But the road can be a bit bumpy at times . . .

David

Twelve-year-old David was scared to death. Summer vacation was over, and he was about to make the transition from sixth to seventh grade—the switch from grade school to junior high.

David had gone to the same school from first grade, and it was a small school: two classes of each grade and only about twenty students in each class.

By the time he was in sixth grade David was well-liked and popular. He did well on the football team, and he was student council president.

David was friendly with everybody, but his group was still made up of the boys in his neighborhood—especially the ones who played football with him day after day, year after year.

Now he and his buddies would be going by bus across town to a junior high, a school that included seventh- through ninth-graders. Instead of forty fellow sixth-graders, David was about to have 400 fellow seventh-graders. About 1,200 students were enrolled at the school.

"I thought it was going to be horrible," David says. "I thought the older kids would pick on me. I didn't think I'd be able to find anybody I knew once they let us off the buses. Who was I going to eat lunch with?"

He didn't know what was going to happen, but he

knew he didn't want to lose his old friends. He didn't want to be alone.

David felt as if he would turn into a nobody.

What Are Friendships?

The friendships you make in grade school are usually a matter of coincidence—in other words, you hang around with kids who live in your neighborhood. Your friends are the kids who live across the street or the people you walk or ride the bus to school with. When you become a teenager or start junior high school, however, friendships are more a matter of choice.

And that may be confusing at first.

Many young people may ask themselves as they move from school to school, "Where do I belong?" There's a good chance that a young person may miss the security he or she had at the smaller school.

In these transitional stages, cliques can be a source of support. But as a young person moves from school to school, does he or she really want to stay with the same group of friends or make new ones?

David Wasn't Alone

David soon realized that he was not alone in his fears; other seventh-graders felt just as he did. But he also discovered that going to junior high school wasn't so bad. He found his buddies at lunch and made a few new friends in classes. In fact, the biggest problem he encountered was figuring out how to work the combination on his locker.

He observed some of the cliques that were already

in existence at the junior high and decided they were not for him. His friends were a combination of his old and new acquaintances, but they were not a cliquish group.

"We're just regular kids that like to joke around a lot . . . you know, we all appreciate a sense of humor," explains David. "And anyone can sit with us at lunch, we don't care. We might gossip a little, but we're not mean."

Questions to Ask Yourself

As you move on to a larger school and look for new friends, school counselors suggest asking yourself the following questions:

- Do you see a clique that seems to have the same interests as you?
- Do clique members seem to be nice to each other?
- Does the group leader seem demanding of group members; for instance, does everyone have to dress the same way?
- What seem to be the good qualities of the clique? Do you see any hints of bad ones?

Remember, however, that if you don't have the qualities some cliques want—no matter how much you want to be part of them—you might be happier with just a couple of friends whom you like and who like you. You'll only be disappointed trying to get into a clique that doesn't want you.

Sometimes cliques are not only about popularity, but also about power. And what gives cliques power?

Power may come from qualities that are automatically

given to a teen—not earned. Coming from a rich family or having good looks are qualities that a teen does not have to earn.

For instance, a teen's parents have money; the teen can afford the expensive clothes that a certain clique expects its members to wear. Is that the kind of group you want to be associated with?

Even though David didn't see a specific clique he wanted to join at his junior high school, he still found friends he enjoyed and could share his thoughts with. For now, he's happy with his situation.

Maryellen

Thirteen-year-old Maryellen had been friends with Jean since kindergarten. They lived next door to each other. They always did everything together—from making cookies to weaving potholders—until they started junior high.

The problem was this: Maryellen had yet to go through any puberty changes, whereas Jean had already developed. She looked like sixteen, but Maryellen, tiny and thin, looked about ten.

Jean had met a group of girls at junior high all of whom had developed as she had. She was more interested in hanging around with this clique who talked about boys and clothes than with Maryellen, who still liked to rent video movies on Friday nights and bake cookies.

Maryellen wasn't ready to think about dating boys. But she missed her friendship with Jean. Because she did look so young, she was being ignored—or snubbed—by many of the students.

One fall day, a day that reminded her of carving

Halloween pumpkins with Jean the year before, Maryellen decided to wait on Jean's front porch and confront her.

As she kicked at the yellow and orange leaves at her feet, Jean came up the sidewalk. She saw Maryellen, and a guilty look came over her face.

"Why don't you like me any more?" Maryellen tried to say calmly. "Why are you ignoring me?"

"I'm not ignoring you; I just have different friends now, Maryellen," Jean said. "I want to do different things than you do. Making cookies and drinking Kool-Aid just isn't exciting enough for me any more, you know what I mean?"

"But . . . but you used to be my best friend!" said Maryellen, her voice beginning to shake and tears forming in her eyes.

"I'm sorry, Maryellen. Maybe when you grow up a little we can be friends again, but for now I'm making new friends and doing different things!"

It Can Be Difficult

Things are not as easy for Maryellen as they are for David. She is still trying to resolve her situation.

Although it's difficult for her to understand what is happening to her friendship with Jean, what she and Jean are experiencing isn't unusual.

Young adolescents mature—physically and emotionally—at different rates. Maryellen need not feel as if she's the only one who's going through this kind of friendship loss, however.

And that's the most important thing to remember: In a situation like Maryellen's you are not alone.

If you are a late bloomer like Maryellen, take a look

around you at school. You'll probably see many different kinds of students in just one classroom.

There will be the boys who have already had a growth spurt and are almost six feet tall, and there will be boys who still look like fourth graders but are really in eighth.

Then there are the girls who are developing—or not developing yet, like Maryellen.

The point is this: In junior high school and even in high school, young people's bodies are changing, but not at the same pace. There are early bloomers and late bloomers. In Maryellen's case the early bloomers formed a clique and shut her out.

Remember, it's okay to make new friends as you move on to new schools, but you shouldn't just forget your old ones. And Jean could have handled her friendship problems with Maryellen a bit better.

Life goes on, of course, but a friend who is moving on to new friendships should try to tell old friends why he or she has decided to spend more time with new acquaintances or cliques.

The best way to settle a dispute or answer a question is to communicate. Everyone involved needs to come to talking terms. Girls, especially, need to go from the crying and screaming stage to the talking stage.

Questions for Troublesome Circumstances

Counselors suggest that old friends discuss the following questions with each other as they move on to new schools and new friends:

- What exactly is the problem you are experiencing? Can you pinpoint it?

- How severe is the problem? One friend might think the problem is worse than others do.
- Is there any way the problem can be solved? Can some kind of compromise be made?

Sara

Sara, who was mentioned in the Introduction, has made the transition from junior high to high school.

Sara still hangs around with her group from junior high, but she wants to make new friends. She's uncomfortable that some of her old friends don't care about their grades and want to try drinking.

She is afraid, however, that she won't be accepted into the group who work on the school newspaper.

A Hard Decision

Sara is in a tough place. She needs to have the strength and courage to let go of her junior high group and to find out more about the newspaper staff. Is this the group she really wants to be associated with while she is in high school?

Sara did find the courage to join the newspaper staff; she told her old friends it was something she wanted to do and she wouldn't have much time to socialize. She was honest with the clique.

There was a lot of talking behind her back at first— "She thinks we're not good enough for her!"—but she felt no loss and more of a sense of relief when she had made her feelings known to the group.

A Glitch for Sara

Sara quickly found out, however, that being on the news staff wasn't as great as it appeared to be. She discovered that some people on the staff didn't feel particularly liked—including herself.

The newspaper adviser, who was a teacher, accepted anyone who wanted to join the staff. However, the various editors had all the power and made all the decisions. The good stories went to those who were part of the "in" clique, the boring stories to the new or disliked staffers.

Sara felt stifled. She screwed up her courage again and visited a yearbook staff meeting. There she found a group of people who really seemed to like each other.

She visited again, and the yearbook staff encouraged her to join and help write copy for the annual. Sara felt no power struggle going on among the yearbook staff, and, most important, she felt comfortable at meetings.

She quit the newspaper staff and joined the yearbook. Although the staff was not as "prestigious" as that of the newspaper in the eyes of most high school students, Sara liked being with them. The newspaper clique was too power-hungry for her tastes.

Making the Decision

As Sara made the transition from junior high to high school, she found she didn't have the freedom to make other friends or undertake other activities because she was so tied into her old clique.

She made the difficult decision to make a break, though, because she didn't want to be tied to that group for the rest of her high school years.

Sara made the break and did not become part of another group right away, although she did join the newspaper staff. She was thus in a good position because—not tied to any particular clique—she could make friends as she wished.

No matter how secure you feel in a clique, if you find you are conforming to what the clique wants you to be, take a closer look at what's going on: Is this where you want to be for the rest of your junior high or high school years?

In any change—whether it's from school to school or group to group—you may feel uncomfortable at first. You might even be lonely at times, but that's part of moving on.

CHAPTER 3

Moving—Leaving
and Starting Over

According to the U.S. Census Bureau, approximately six million young people move with their families each year.

So if a parent announces that he or she has taken a better or different job in another town, don't feel alone. Remember, those six million other young people are packing boxes too.

Says Greg Knoll, a counselor at a Colorado high school with 1,200 students, "Lots of kids move a lot . . . parents move where the money, the jobs are. Parents are moving at all times of the year with no consideration for the kids: They'll move a kid who's a senior, or they'll leave a kid behind. It's tough on kids. . . . [The kids] always have to start over, and the older you are, the harder it is."

Moving into a new community is not only hard on a teen but on the entire family. Everyone loses something.

What can young people do to make the best of this situation? Understanding the emotions that come with a move is a necessity, and teens should try to make the move a positive experience, not a negative one.

The move will be tough, especially if you're leaving a place where you have lived your whole life. But don't think of the move as a negative experience that is causing you to lose friends. That's not the right attitude.

Think positively: Think of the new friends you can make. School counselors say that moving can be an opportunity to rethink your life and make changes. You can think about who you want to be in your new town.

For instance, are you ready to change your image from shy to outgoing? No one will know that you used to be afraid to raise your hand and answer a question in class. No one will know that you always used to look down when you passed popular people in the halls.

Are you being pressured by your clique to skip school or do other things you don't want to do? Change! After your family moves, hook up with new acquaintances who have higher aspirations than your old gang.

Young people who have moved around a lot since they were toddlers know about the opportunities for change. When boys or girls have to go it alone at new schools time after time, they learn to become more self-sufficient. They learn how to cope and make new friends easily.

And they have learned through experience that an optimistic, positive attitude helps make each move easier.

Sally

Sally, now eighteen, moved from one Minneapolis neighborhood to the next as a toddler and child. While she was in grade school, her family moved to Texas, then New Mexico. Her family finally settled in Colorado when she was a junior in high school.

Her parents were loving, creative free spirits and tried many locations and different occupations. Moving became a way of life for Sally. All in all, she lived in sixteen neighborhoods in four states. Making new friends every time her family moved became a way of life for her too.

"I was never *really* popular—I always moved away before I had a chance," Sally says. However, she always had two or three good friends in every place she lived. She learned to be accepting of different cultures and new life-styles. One of her friends was terribly overweight, "but she was a neat person and one of the best friends I ever had," Sally says.

"'New' always meant 'good' to me," she explains. Moving was always a chance to meet new people and experience new groups. And one time "good" was especially true.

Always an excellent student who followed her parents' rules, during her sophomore year in high school in Santa Fe, Sally became part of a clique that was cutting classes and drinking. She also was being pressured to have sex with one of the boys in the group.

Then in the summer her family decided to move to the Colorado mountains. Sally felt some relief. She knew her reputation would be hard to clean up in Santa Fe, but the move to Colorado would give her a chance to start fresh and become a serious student again.

Once in Colorado, she became interested in photography—there was plenty of scenery to take pictures of—and she joined the new school's magazine staff as a photographer.

Through that group, Sally made friends with the

same interests, but they also taught her about enjoying the outdoors. Hiking, not drinking, was what many of her new friends liked to do.

Charlotte

Charlotte, nineteen, whose father is with the U.S. Forest Service, is an only child. Growing up, she lived in five states and more than twenty neighborhoods.

"I was always an outgoing child—I had to be to make new friends," Charlotte says.

"I have found that I enjoy associating and working with others. To this day, I can be alone and still feel comfortable while other kids always seem to need someone with them constantly. They can never bear to be alone—going to the bathroom or going to their lockers.

"Being an only child and moving around a lot taught me to rely on myself and not others for my own security."

Because Charlotte was comfortable with herself, she could easily eat alone in the cafeteria. "I didn't have to eat at a designated table with a designated group."

She also became tolerant of all types of social groups. In junior high and high school, she "dated cowboys, punkers, jocks, presidents of student councils—all kinds."

Charlotte says she has always had a deep curiosity about people, so she tried out different groups but didn't automatically join them.

"I never judged anybody, but I was never taken in [by bad groups]," she explains. "I never had any enemies because I tried to understand why each group did what they did."

Chris

Chris, on the other hand, moved as often as Charlotte and Sally but ended up frustrated with moving. His father was a high-ranking officer in the Air Force, which caused the family to be transferred from base to base.

When Chris was fourteen his parents split up, and he was shuffled between his father and mother. He tired of moving. He also tired of living with his father for a few months, then with his mother for the next few months. By the time he was a junior in high school he had become withdrawn and his grades went down.

In the past Chris had always tried to be part of the popular group. But that was no longer where he wanted to be. His parents were having financial problems because of their divorce, and the popular groups usually required that you have the right clothes and plenty of cash on hand to go to a movie or pizza restaurant—whatever the activity for the day might be.

Chris just wanted to be himself.

He ended up with his mother in California for his last year of high school and didn't try to fit in with the "in" crowd.

"A lot of the people were stuck up . . . I didn't waste my time with them," he says.

Instead, he joined a group of students who were called "skaters." Chris spent a lot of time watching them manipulate their skateboards around the school grounds. The skaters noticed him watching and started friendly conversations with him.

Although skateboarding had originally brought the group together, Chris says he found that this clique of young men and women "let me be me." And they weren't stupid either. They had fun, but they also studied.

Indirectly, his new clique helped Chris feel confident about himself because they accepted him as he was. They also shared the same values: Good times were important, but so were good grades.

Studies show that it takes a new student an average of twenty-three days to make new friends.

But young people who are moving for the first time should be aware that it is usually the "bad" crowds that are the least judgmental and will accept just about anybody right away; you don't have to be popular or known to get in.

The adjective "bad" is defined differently by different people. For instance, "bad" students may skip school, smoke joints, or be in car-theft rings, or they may just have negative attitudes toward schoolwork.

Since "bad" groups will accept you immediately, you may be tempted to hang around with these cliques just because you are feeling lonely. But remember, you'll eventually have to deal with leaving the group. If you know in your heart that these are not people you really want to be friends with, don't join up with them.

Also, keep in mind that when you choose your peer group you are choosing your reputation. What group—if any—do you want to be identified with?

When you arrive at your new junior high or high

school, open your eyes. Check which groups are the most popular. What students are in the group?

Take your time.

If you are alone for a while right after a move, it can be a time for looking at yourself and learning what you want out of life—not what a clique wants from you. Keep busy doing things for yourself.

As you prepare to move, here is a list of things to do or to think about suggested by school counselors:

- Plan to keep in touch with your old friends if you want to, but don't let your old life get in the way of making new friends. Look ahead; don't dwell on the past.
- What activities, if any, do you want to try at your new location? Is it time to give football, basketball, track, or cheerleading a try?
- What does "success" mean to you now that you've moved? Good grades? Lots of friends? A part-time job?
- What qualities do you want to change with this move? Attitude? Appearance? Start a list!
- Instead of being mad at your parents about moving, talk to them about your fears. They'll probably share some of theirs with you.

Jep Enck, who is a former junior high teacher, says that young people need to be more selective in choosing friends after a move.

"Some take the path of least resistance," Enck says. "They may become friends with someone just because their lockers are next to each other. Explore the groups . . . Give yourself a mental visitor's pass to visit the cliques, the school organizations."

No matter when you move—at the beginning, middle, or end of the school year—there are always advantages.

If you move in the middle of a year you can get involved in classes and other school activities right away. If you move at the beginning of the summer, it may be more difficult to meet other teens your age, but you'll have all summer to decide what you want to pursue when the new school year begins.

Some young people, however, don't want to move at midyear, especially if they are seniors in high school.

Consider your options if you find yourself in a midyear move. You might be able to stay with a friend, a relative, or another responsible adult until the end of the school year. But also consider what's best for you. Will you be so homesick and miss your family so much that you'll be too distracted to finish out the school year?

If you move on with your family, however, evaluate yourself, make some improvements, and take time to find a group of friends that you're comfortable with.

CHAPTER 4

Dealing with Pressure from Cliques

Cliques have their good qualities, say adolescent counselors and other experts. Cliques help teens learn about other teens and their beliefs, and a person who belongs to one usually has some kind of social life.

And within a clique, there can actually be good peer pressure. For instance, teens might ask other clique members to attend church or an alcohol-free party with them.

However, there are those cliques that have only bad peer pressure qualities, and they have the power to influence young peoples' behavior in negative ways.

For example, some cliques may expect young people to be mean to others, to participate in "people-bashing," or to undertake illegal or dangerous activities such as using or selling drugs.

Young people may stop making decisions on their own. They may conform to what the group wants them to do and be. They no longer can decide right and wrong on their own.

For some young people, usually those with low self-esteem, it's sometimes easier to conform to what the clique is doing. If they do something that goes against the clique, it means taking the risk of being considered *different*—which is a situation some teens don't want to handle.

You need to make your choices based on what is right for you, not what is right for your pals. Some cliques will ignore you or put you down if you don't always do what their members want you to do.

So what is more important? Membership in a clique? Or being comfortable with your decisions?

Todd

Todd, a native of Denver, was shy and a loner throughout grade school. He read a lot and had a lot to say, but he never had the opportunity to share his thoughts with others. Until ninth grade.

In his last year of junior high, Todd met Joey in computer class. They sat next to each other for a few periods, then they started talking. They discovered that they had the same video game systems and many of the same games.

Joey suggested that Todd come to a video arcade with his group after school. Todd agreed, and he soon met four of Joey's friends. He found it easy to talk with all of them, and for once in his life he felt he really wanted to belong to a clique. They happily took him in.

"I have to admit that we were really nerds, you know, into computers and electronics and things like that," explained Todd a few years later at the age of twenty. "But we had each other, and that was cool. We all wore long coats, and we called ourselves the Wizards. Joey was the head wizard."

And Joey liked control. After a few weeks of hanging around with the Wizards, Todd realized that Joey wanted the group to do what he wanted them to do, and that wasn't always going to a video arcade. It was trying different drugs or drinking beer at lunch.

Unfortunately, Todd was still so happy to be part of a group and have others to talk with that he went along with whatever Joey wanted.

By junior high graduation, Todd realized that Joey's influence was having a bad effect. He had started to cut classes, and he wasn't studying at all. Joey had told them they were above all that—they were too smart to be bothered with schoolwork.

By the end of the summer Todd and Joey had tried just about everything there was to try in the way of drugs. Todd did not enjoy the summer, and he lived in fear of being caught.

High school days were just around the corner, however, and when school started the Wizards formed their group again.

Todd went to classes and actually had a few that he thought he would probably enjoy—creative writing, drama, and another computer course. But he never found out. The Wizards decided—after encouragement from Joey—that they would not go to school any more. Instead, they would walk around different parts of Denver each day, using mind-altering drugs and deciding the fate of the world—or at least the fate of their lives. Such mind-expanding conversations would be more helpful than school could ever be, Joey explained.

Todd started to worry. This was going to be the same as dropping out of school. Was that what he really wanted? What was he to do? If he told Joey that he didn't want to skip school every day, that they should attend classes every now and then, he knew Joey would reject him and then the others would too.

He'd be a loner again, and he didn't want that. He liked belonging to a group.

Taking a Stand

Todd's problem from the start of his relationship with the Wizards was that he was always too willing to say yes to whatever the clique wanted to do.

He should have done some healthy arguing—even about little things such as the kind of pizza they ordered. He should have shown the Wizards that he had opinions of his own.

If he had broken the ice and argued with Joey, maybe the other Wizards would have too. Maybe everyone would have started expressing opinions.

If you find yourself in a situation like Todd's, you can change or gain control of your own life if you want to—even though it may not be easy.

Look at your flaws or weaknesses. First, how do you act? Do you make friends easily? Do you have your own opinions? Do you like yourself? If you answer yes to those questions, peer pressure probably is not a problem for you. And if you know what you believe in—and your group is not pressuring you to act or think differently—your clique has a positive quality.

If, however, you're pressured to go against what you believe in, you'll get out of such a clique. You'll need a strong self-image, though.

Resisting the Pressure

Todd knew that if he didn't go along with the Wizards, Joey would talk behind his back and they would make his life miserable. He felt threatened by loneliness and possible ridicule if he didn't walk the streets of Denver with the Wizards every day.

So why was Todd giving in, even though he had doubts?

Joey was actually using "emotional blackmail." For Todd and the other Wizards, Joey had made their lives seem meaningless unless they were sharing it with—or giving it to—their clique.

According to Leslie Kaplan in her book *Coping with Peer Pressure*, those who join a group to learn from it will leave if they are pressured; however, those who join a group to become popular or just to belong will stay and do what they really don't want to—like Todd.

Kaplan says the fear of rejection by the group upsets some young people more than the inner anxiety, dissatisfaction, and mixed feelings they experience about what they are doing: At least with the group they are not alone.

And that is what Todd was experiencing. *92- /8547*

Todd Needed Strength

Todd eventually was kicked out of school. And when he returned to school, he didn't go back to his old high school; instead, he finished his education at an alternative high school.

Todd had been a loner for such a long time that after he joined the Wizards he didn't want to return to those lonely junior high days again.

He never gave himself a chance, however, to find out what group, if any, he really belonged in.

Maybe he would have discovered that he would never fit into one special clique. He might have found one or two friends that he could have had fun with.

Todd also was being picked on by Joey; he needed more strength, greater self-esteem. He needed to talk himself out of the loser role he had put himself in.

Although Todd liked the security of a group, he also felt a need to be his independent self. He really did want to show up at some of his high school classes that sounded interesting. He wanted to learn things other than what his clique was teaching him.

There were ways Todd could have refused some of the activities that Joey wanted him to participate in. He could have told his friends that he had something else to do. He could have avoided those high-risk situations where he might be pressured into doing something he didn't want to do.

Not having a mind of your own does nothing for your self-respect; therefore, you shouldn't let others control your actions. People won't respect you if you are always a "yes" person, so be yourself!

Remember, you really don't like everyone, so why do you want everyone to like you?

Not everyone can be your friend.

CHAPTER 5

Getting into a Clique and Making New Friends

A person's teen years may be the most cliquish time of his or her life.

When do you ever see a teen alone? Not very often. Teens walk together at the mall or downtown, they drive around in groups, they go to movies or rock concerts in groups, and they're always eating together in fast-food places or in the cafeteria.

As mentioned earlier, cliques have their good points. In their clique teenagers have a place, they're not alone, and they learn how to get along with others.

Sometimes, however, young people find that they want to try something different. The clique they belong to is in a rut; everyone does the same old thing all the time.

Young people may have new ideas or new activities

they want to try, and their clique is holding them back. Maybe it's time to make new friends.

That does not necessarily mean losing old friends. It can mean widening your circle of acquaintances.

Marti

Marti, sixteen, was tired of going to the mall every Saturday. But that's what her clique did every weekend, and nobody else seemed to mind or want to change. She wished that her group would do something different for a change.

In the cafeteria at lunch time, Marti's group usually discussed what they had bought the weekend before at the mall, what they were going to buy the next time they went to the mall, what they were going to wear to the mall, and whom they hoped to see at the mall.

The mall, the mall, the mall! Marti could have screamed.

She liked her girlfriends—they were like family— but she realized that she was becoming less and less interested in what they liked to do.

Then Marti's mother gave her a catalog of courses offered through the city's Parks and Recreation Department. Several art classes were offered on Saturdays. There was an all-afternoon pottery workshop coming up for those sixteen years old and older.

Marti had always enjoyed being creative and working with her hands. She decided she would enroll in the course. No more Saturdays at the mall!

Her friends were disappointed at first, but they had to admit that Marti hadn't been much fun during recent mall outings. Once in her class, however, Marti made them all little pottery bowls as a sign of her continued friendship. They actually seemed to admire her, and one girl asked her how she had found out about the pottery course.

In the meantime, Marti made new friends—Jodi and Tim—through her Saturday classes. They were both seventeen and attended a different high school, but they shared Marti's interest in art.

After pottery workshop, the three of them began stopping for a snack and to talk about what they were going to create the next Saturday.

Jodi and Tim knew about all kinds of art, and Marti was learning a lot from them. They all hoped to major in art in college some day.

Through Jodi and Tim, Marti met other young people who were interested in the creative arts. She went to a few parties with them and was amazed to meet so many teens who were such individualists, so much themselves.

These people wore what they wanted to and had interests in so many different things—from musical groups to books.

Grow or Go?

In a clique everyone needs to grow together, and if members seem ready to grow in different directions, trouble can start.

Marti felt that she was not learning anything from her group and was beginning to lose her individuality.

But Marti's group, after a period of adjustment, allowed her to grow and meet new people. They remained her friends; she still saw them at school and ate lunch with them. They started to show an interest in her outside activities.

Although Marti's weekend plans were different from the clique's, she maintained a nice balance between her old and new friends.

Young people sometimes fail to realize that it's okay to be a member of several cliques. They can participate in different activities with different groups.

When you're looking at your clique and thinking about trying new ones, consider some questions: Are you losing your individuality by staying with your clique? Are the friendships that you have in your clique still meaningful? Are you bored?

When teens choose a peer group, they are choosing their reputation. That's why it's so important to find a group of friends with whom you feel comfortable. Get out and visit other groups!

If you're in a group where you're not stimulated or not having any fun, maybe it's time to go exploring.

Young people who are in a group or are checking out new ones should "tune in to their bodies," says Jep Enck. "Your body is smarter than your brain sometimes."

While you're with a group, consider the following questions:

- Am I smiling or frowning?
- Does my stomach feel good or upset? (Am I tense?)
- What does the group expect of me?
- In general, do I feel comfortable?
- Did I have to give up friends to join this group?
- Do they accept me for what I am or for what they can get from me?
- Are their values the same as mine?

- Do I really want to be known as part of this group? (Is its reputation something I can live with?)

Here's an analogy: You're outside on a winter day. You tense up, especially in your shoulders and neck, because you are so cold. Finally you get to go into your warm house. Your body relaxes and you feel much better.

If you're in a group and you're feeling tense and uncomfortable, come in out of the cold! Find a place where it's nice and warm. Find a group or a couple of friends with whom you're comfortable.

But how do you go about using this imaginary visitor's pass? How do you go about meeting new folks?

Obviously, you have to take the first step.

As a sort of exercise, counselors suggest choosing someone you know nothing about and introducing yourself—perhaps at the beginning or end of the school day or during free time after lunch. Spend some time talking with him or her. If the person doesn't want to talk to you, at least you've tried.

If you have time for after-school activities, school clubs and organizations usually need people. Many junior highs and high schools provide a variety of activities from Students Against Drunk Driving (SADD) to the pep club to the ski club.

There may be citywide programs you could get involved in—as Marti did. If you belong to a church, see what activities it offers for its teenagers.

Remember that friends will always form around certain activities, whether academic, social, or athletic.

As mentioned earlier, the potential always exists for power-hungry cliques in school or city-sponsored clubs, so you may have to try a couple before you find one that fits.

Your main goal is to get in touch with people who share your interests or who can teach you something new. And although finding the right group or the right friends is important to all teens, remember that it can take time.

You may not find a compatible clique immediately because you don't know yet what your real interests are. Evaluate your situation. Maybe you just don't belong with a certain clique, no matter how appealing it looks.

When you think you've found a clique that's right for you, make sure that it sees you as an equal, it respects your opinions, and it's fun! And your gang should be able to accept that you might have friends outside of the group.

It's natural to be worried about making friends, but making the effort is a good thing—you're learning to get along with others. You can have a "visitor's pass" throughout your life.

Remember, the world is not full of strangers, it is full of potential friends.

CHAPTER 6

Getting Out of
a Clique

Young people often find themselves in a clique they don't like just because that clique happens to be the one that accepted them.

Cliques can be snobbish and can keep their members from meeting others. As mentioned earlier, certain cliques exert peer pressure to participate in activities that a teen doesn't really want to do: shoplifting, drinking, using drugs.

Some teens stay with such cliques because they think it's better to belong to a group than not to have any attachments. Others, however, find that it's time to get out.

Jeff

Jeff's parents both had good jobs. His dad was an officer at a bank, and his mother was the manager of a prestigious clothing store. The family had no money problems.

Jeff, a sophomore, always had nice clothes to wear, and on his recent sixteenth birthday his parents had bought him a car—not a brand-new one, but a Ford Mustang that was in great shape.

Since the beginning of tenth grade, Jeff's friends had been other teens whose parents were well off. His group never worried about having money for movies or hamburgers after school. In fact, none of them had afterschool or weekend jobs.

No snob himself, Jeff considered his group somewhat snobbish on the whole. But it was his clique, and so far he felt comfortable enough hanging around with them.

In January, when a new quarter started, Jeff ended up sitting next to a boy named Andy in English class.

Andy came from a broken home and lived with his mother, who worked as a teller at the bank where Jeff's father was an executive.

Andy worked at a fast-food restaurant after school— in fact, at the one where Jeff and his friends went for after-school snacks.

Andy, his ten-year-old brother, and his mother lived in a small apartment in what Jeff's group would consider "the bad part of town."

Sitting together in English class, they began to talk to each other. Jeff enjoyed Andy's quick wit and sense of humor; in fact, he had never met anyone as funny as Andy. Jeff also admired him because even though he worked a part-time job he got good grades.

Jeff enjoyed Andy so much that he wanted to spend more time with him outside of class. One day, he asked Andy to come over and eat lunch with him and his friends.

When Andy showed up with his tray, Jeff's friends

stopped talking and looked at each other. Jeff introduced Andy all around, and everyone managed a "Hi," but the atmosphere was uncomfortable. Jeff's friends were obviously snubbing Andy.

Jeff and Andy finished their meals and walked outside.

"Hey, your friends are snobs," Andy said. "Just because I don't have a car and fancy clothes—and I serve them their stupid burgers every afternoon—they think I'm not good enough to sit with them."

Jeff quickly said: "That's not true! I don't know what's wrong with them today. Usually they're a lot of fun."

"Yeah, a barrel of laughs," Andy said. "I don't need to hang around that kind of stuck-up people, even if they are your so-called friends."

Jeff was both embarrassed by and mad at his clique. He realized that having Andy as a friend was important. He also realized that his clique might not be the great group he thought it was.

Jeff came to realize that he was spending all his time with people he didn't approve of any more: His clique was too judgmental. At the beginning of sophomore year Jeff had automatically joined it because his family had moved into an upper-middle-class neighborhood where members of the group lived. Jeff was good-looking, well dressed, and easily accepted by the group.

Perhaps Jeff didn't use his best judgment when he joined the clique, because now he found himself unhappy and wanted to quit.

But that's easier said than done.

Consequences of Leaving

What may happen if Jeff tries to leave the clique? He may be lonely and on his own for a while (although Andy would probably become a friend). Or he may find that the clique won't want to let him go.

Some peer groups don't like members to make friends outside. Jeff's clique showed a low tolerance level for outsiders. His friendliness with Andy was considered betrayal. They began to treat him differently. He knew they were talking behind his back. One member, Alex, told him to stop hanging around with "white trash." Jeff was getting pressure to "remain loyal" to his group.

If you're thinking of leaving your clique, consider how its members have been treating you. If you're embarrassed by them, as Jeff was, or if they're making you feel bad, maybe it's time to change.

Jeff did drop out of his clique. He found that his so-called popularity was not worth preserving. He had the courage to move on.

It was difficult for him to do, however. Most of the members lived in his neighborhood; he still saw them frequently, and they snubbed him if he said "Hi."

But Jeff felt okay; he found that he didn't need to be just like everyone in a certain clique.

Remember, what you do is up to you—from the way you dress to the activities you choose. Rosalind Jones, a junior high school counselor, says that if you have a friend or a clique you don't want to hang around with for any reason, just don't hang around them. But don't run away.

"Face the problem, but do what you have to do," she says. "Maybe do some role-playing before you leave; pretend you are leaving the group."

Rehearsing what you will tell the group when you are

ready to leave may help you feel more confident when the time comes to announce your departure.

It's very important for you to give your explanation; if you don't, the group will have even more reason to gossip behind your back.

Getting Out

Cliques can exert strong peer pressure. If the members of your clique are drinking every weekend, experimenting with pot, and skipping school, what are you going to do? Do you really want to participate in those activities?

If you're in a clique and your grades fall, school counselors say it's time to check out the reasons. If they fall a little, okay; however, a steep drop is not okay. Ask yourself just how far you're willing to go to stay with a clique that is not helping your future.

Some cliques have the reputation of being a group of "hoods." When these teens become destructive or violent, however, they are called gangs. Is that the image you want to project? That of a gang member?

Remember that a clique can be a support system, but it also can pressure teens into doing things they might not otherwise do.

Pat Nash, a high school counselor, says that smart students may start hanging around with teens who skip school or show other inappropriate behavior.

"Then they get stuck . . . it's too hard for them to get a new group of peers.

"But it's up to the students to make the change, and if they don't make a change, it originates from a lack of security somewhere."

For instance, Bert, a high school junior, says he wants to do well in school, but he hangs around with some teens who brag about flunking out and not doing their homework.

If Bert were a leader in the clique, he could influence the others to start attending classes again; however, as just one of the members chances are no one will listen to him. He has to decide on his own what to do: Stay or go?

You're Not a Quitter, You Were a "Try-er"

So you've tried the group, and now you're uncomfortable. Don't make yourself miserable. You can get out. Quit because you don't like the group. Give yourself a pat on the back for having tried in the first place. You're not a quitter, you were a "try-er."

If you're bored or don't really know why you are in the group, see what others are doing. Move on to friends or groups who really care about you.

You may have to break away from your friends to save yourself, and if you're really having a hard time detaching yourself from a group, you may have to seek professional help. (See Chapter 15.) Talk to your parents.

But *you* have to decide what you need to do.

After you break away, you'll probably keep running into your old friends. That may make you uncomfortable. Try to get into classes that they're not in, or switch study halls if necessary. Ask your school counselor what you can do.

If you can't get away from your old clique in school, then at least try when you're away from school. Community centers, parks and rec programs, church groups, college student centers, pools, gyms, and health clubs all offer classes or activities; there are lots of places besides school to meet people.

Being part of a group doesn't guarantee happiness, and

realize too that not all friendships last: People find new interests, new priorities. There's some pain involved in change, but take the good memories—if there are any—and move on, get out.

Nothing is wrong with having a crowd of friends. It's when the clique becomes too judgmental of others or too closed-minded that it's time to do a reality check.

Cliques are like displays in a candy store. You have a right to choose.

CHAPTER 7

Friends of Many Colors

Adrian and Michael

Adrian was an eighteen-year-old Hispanic youth who grew up in a small town in southern Colorado. When he graduated from high school, all his classmates were Hispanic, and so was his girlfriend.

That fall, however, he left the security of his small town and entered a state university a couple of hundred miles away. The university town had a population of 100,000.

Adrian's dormitory roommate, Michael, was of Italian descent and from New York City. Adrian was not sure how Michael—or anyone—would treat him once he got to school.

Michael was cool to Adrian at first. But one night, after the two had been studying silently at their desks for hours, they began to talk.

First they talked about their classes, how difficult they were and how much studying there was to do. Then the conversation moved on to other matters college freshman face, such as making friends and finding fun.

Finally Michael said, "Hey, Adrian, you're not so bad. You have to realize where I come from, man. New York City. A big Italian neighborhood. My friends are very racist. If blacks or Hispanics come into our neighborhood, that is not appreciated, if you know what I mean?"

"Oh, yeah," Adrian said. "I've always hung around Hispanics. My mom has already told me that I have to marry a Mexican girl to keep the culture alive, you know? But what if I come home with a white girl? That could easily happen now that I'm away from home, going to school with all kinds of people."

"Yeah, really," Michael said. "You know, we'll be spending a lot of time together in this room. We'll probably become good friends. What if one of us wants to take the other back to our old stomping grounds? What would happen then?"

America is called a melting pot; our country is made up of many ethnic groups. For example, there are Americans with their roots in Mexico, Puerto Rico, and Asia; there are Jews, Italians, Irish, Poles, Afro-Americans, and Native Americans. All these people and their cultures combine to create our unique country.

Many of our colleges, high schools, and junior high schools represent a broad range of cultures. And teens who accept the fact and make friends from other heritages benefit doubly: Not only do they have friends, but they have friends from whom they can learn new things. They can learn about the food, music, dance, and holiday customs of a different culture. They can even learn a little history along the way.

Many young people are unaccepting of other races. But as seventeen-year-old Jeff Arnett says in a recent *Parade Magazine* article, "I don't know how we're going to learn to deal with all this. But I think it's up to us. The more our generation associates with each other, the more unscared of each other we'll get. And once that happen, things will get better."

Adrian and Michael did become good friends, and they did visit each other's hometowns. Adrian went to New York, and Michael went to southern Colorado, and they both learned a lot.

Michael hiked through the open fields and foothills where Adrian had grown up, and Adrian rode the subway to visit the landmarks of the Big Apple. Michael enjoyed trying the spicy foods that Adrian's mother prepared for them. He tried dishes of green and red chiles; he tried tamales and sopaipillas. He loved it all. Adrian, on the other hand, got a taste of some of the best Italian tomato sauces and pasta dishes.

The boys' parents and old friends, after seeing the good relationship between the roommates, eventually got past their prejudices. A certain respect was created.

During many a late-night conversation, however, the boys had decided that their old friends and those old ways were something that could be left behind. Luckily, the old ways were left behind, but their old friends were not.

Kayla

Kayla, a black high school junior who was a good student and also a cheerleader, was asked to the prom by the star basketball player, Josh, a senior who happened to be white.

Kayla's and Josh's friendship had grown over the school year, and they often found themselves talking to each other at parties after basketball games and when they ran into each other in the halls at school.

They were attracted to each other, so it seemed natural to attend the prom together. Their friends at school thought it was natural too. If someone asked Kayla who she was going to prom with and she said Josh, the next question was merely, "What are you going to wear?"

Josh's friends were very accepting too. They discussed where Josh was taking his date to dinner on prom night and that was about all.

It was no big deal.

For Josh's and Kayla's parents, however, it *was* a big deal. Josh's mother had a fit, screaming that Kayla was not good enough for him.

Josh was furious. Kayla was very smart, he told his mother; she probably got better grades than he did!

Josh's father basically stayed out of the argument but said that Josh should attend the prom with whomever he wished. That made Josh's mother even more furious.

At Kayla's house the reaction was similar. "Why can't you date one of the black players on the team?" her mother asked.

"What's the difference?" asked Kayla. "We're all

people! What does it matter what color Josh's skin is?"

Kayla also asked why her single mother could have white and Hispanic friends, but when Kayla decided to date someone of a different color her mom became a hypocrite.

The atmosphere was not pleasant in Kayla's household, and her younger sisters listened in amazement to the arguments—this was what they'd be up against soon if they considered dating white boys.

Kayla and Josh at first were afraid to admit to each other their families' reactions. But each one knew that something was bothering the other, and they began to talk about it after school one afternoon. The prom was two weeks off.

"My mom is really upset that I'm going to the prom with you, Josh," Kayla said, trying to keep her voice from shaking. "She thinks you'll take advantage of me because I'm black or something. I don't know. It's hard for me to understand her thinking."

Josh sighed and explained his situation. "My mom is freaking out too," he said. "Dad is being cool about it, so now Mom's not only mad at me but at him too! We've got to do something about this mess."

Kayla and Josh decided to act like adults and stop arguing with their mothers. Instead, they decided to set up meetings with each mother so they could calmly state their case.

After meeting Kayla, Josh's mother agreed that she was a nice, well-educated girl; however, she still didn't approve of Josh's taking her to the prom. She remained prejudiced.

Kayla's mother liked Josh too, and she liked how he paid attention to her younger daughters, treating them with respect and asking them questions about themselves. Kayla's mom gave in.

Kayla and Josh went to the prom together. Josh's mother didn't speak to him the entire weekend. His father, however, stood by him. In fact, as he handed Josh the car keys on prom night he whispered, "Don't worry about your mother. I know her. It may take time, but she'll get over this. If she thinks you're happy, that's all that matters."

Josh and Kayla did continue to date after the dance. Josh went away to college in the fall, but they continued to write and call each other. By the next Christmas, when Kayla came by Josh's house to visit, his mother had become accepting of their situation. But it had taken many months for her to become "colorblind."

In America, many people still have prejudices. Young people may hear insensitive comments at home such as, "Why don't they go back where they came from?" That is not realistic; in the melting pot of America, almost everyone would have to leave the country.

If young people learn to be proud of their country's cultural and ethnic diversity—and learn from that diversity—perhaps they can help show those who are still prejudiced that everyone should be treated as a human being.

Unfortunately, hate crimes are growing in America, and many of the crimes are being committed by teens.

According to a 1991 *Scholastic Update* article on violent youth, almost all minority groups in the United States report an increase in "bias crimes."

Attacks on blacks and gays are up, as is violence against

Jews, Asians, Hispanics, and Arab Americans. Some of the most violent crimes are committed by "skinheads," young people who believe in white supremacy.

Why an increase in "people-bashing" by teens? It's a way to feel a part of a clique. They band together and decide that they will be against others who are not like them.

Racism is a problem in the 1990s. Before teens join a clique where people-bashing is a favorite pastime, they should look inside themselves: Are they just pretending to be racists? Is this really how they want to act toward other human beings?

CHAPTER 8

Why You Wear What You Wear

Leeann

Ninth-grader Leeann and her small clique of girl-friends liked to think that they were nonconformists and not materialistic in any way. They wore clothes they liked, not clothes that had a "label."

Leeann and her friends took physical education together with quite a few girls who were obsessed with "label" dressing. These girls wore expensive clothing made by Esprit or Benetton and looked down on those who didn't.

Also in the gym class were several girls from lower-income families who couldn't afford to wear "label" clothing even if they wanted to.

As the first semester continued, the "label" dressers acted superior to those who did not wear what was "cool." They looked at the others in the gym class with distaste, raising their eyes and making tsk-tsk sounds.

Toward the end of the semester, Leeann decided to do something about these girls' attitudes; she didn't want to be cruel, but she wanted to make a point.

She bought little mailing labels and printed "Esprit" on dozens of them. The next day—the last gym class of the semester—as everyone was changing back to street clothes, Leeann went to her friends and the others who didn't wear name brands and gave them "Esprit" stickers to put all over their clothing.

Then they all paraded by the snobs with big smiles and comments such as "See you next semester."

What Leeann did was not mean, but she made a point: Why do we all have to wear labels? Were the snobbish girls wearing certain clothing just to please their peers or so they could hang around a certain group?

Why can't teens dress to please themselves?

Most teens, as they get older, do find their own identity when it comes to clothing and style, but while they search for that identity they often choose to wear what members of their clique are wearing.

Often, however, clothing is not a matter of choice in a clique: teens *must* dress a certain way or wear certain brands to be accepted. If they don't, they're not "cool," and the rest of the members don't want to hang around with them.

Experimenting

More innocent perhaps are the styles a clique may try out as a group. Perhaps a group decides to mimic the tie-dye,

Indian-print, hippie look of the 1960s. No one is pressured to go along; everyone just experiments.

Another group may decide to wear all black, and it's up to each member to come up with his or her own definition of "all black." Perhaps one person will wear black socks, shoes, pants, and shirt and then go a step further and dye his or her brown or blond hair black. A girl member may merely wear a black skirt and shoes and accent the outfit with brightly colored hose and sweater. The look is up to the individual.

Experimentation helps young people find their own unique styles.

However, it's when teens are pressured to wear what others are wearing that a problem arises.

Unless young people truly want to—and can afford to—wear a certain kind of clothing, they should question the values their cliques are placing on them before they rush out and buy new wardrobes. Is this style or brand-name obsession really for them?

Harry

Thirteen-year-old Harry begged and begged his parents to buy him a Miami Dolphins warm-up jacket. A couple of his friends had such jackets, and some of the cooler kids in his junior high wore them too.

Harry's parents couldn't understand his sudden interest in the Miami Dolphins or in football jackets. Harry was a basketball nut. To them he seemed obsessed with this piece of clothing.

The jackets cost well over $100, but his parents finally gave in and said they would give him one for his birthday.

Harry lived in a large city on the East Coast. His city—and in fact, his school—had a large population of poor people. There had been some after-school encounters in which boys from the poorer neighborhoods had taken baseball caps or other items of clothing from kids who were walking home alone or in pairs. Harry never thought much about the incidents, however. He rode the bus to school, and it let him off not too far from his house. Many of his friends traveled with him too.

Finally Harry's birthday came, and he got his jacket. He wore it proudly to school the next day. His friends were favorably impressed, and for a few days he got a lot of attention.

A week later, Harry missed the bus home. That meant he had to walk, but it wasn't too far, about two miles.

He started out, but after a few blocks he felt uneasy. He looked back and saw five boys his age following him. They all had on black baseball caps with some team logo. He didn't recognize any of them.

Harry began to walk faster; he was worried. He wished he wasn't wearing his new jacket; he thought maybe that's what they wanted.

Unfortunately for Harry, that was what they wanted. The gang caught up with him beside a park. They chased him into a secluded area and demanded the jacket. At first he refused, but they continued to threaten him, and one boy pulled out a switch-blade knife.

Harry took off the jacket and handed it over. The boy put the switch-blade away, and the group ran off through the park. Harry could hear them laughing.

*   *   *

Today, clothing as a status symbol has reached epidemic proportions, especially in large cities where many cliques sport certain brands of sportswear or shoes.

Harry, though not in a gang, wanted the jacket as a status symbol because he thought he would be more popular. And for a couple of days he was. But should he try to buy popularity with a faddish, expensive jacket? Is that right?

More and more young people are resorting to violence to get the trendy clothes they want but can't afford: a certain brand of shoes, a baseball cap, or a leather jacket.

Harry learned a lesson. And he was lucky too. Other young people have not been so lucky. A fifteen-year-old boy in Maryland was strangled by a friend with whom he played basketball. Why? His friend wanted his Air Jordan basketball shoes.

Because of such incidents many schools now forbid students to wear certain kinds of clothing on campus. And some parents refuse to buy or allow their children to buy clothing that might put their lives in jeopardy.

Having high self-esteem will help teens deal with any kind of clothing conflict. Material things such as Esprit clothing or a football jacket can't express a teen's personality as well as a positive self-image can.

CHAPTER ◇ 9

What About Gangs?

Gary

When Gary was sixteen and seventeen he played basketball for his high school, which was a large one in a Mid-western city. He was pretty good too. As a sophomore he was second-string, but as a junior when he was seventeen he got to play first-string.

While Gary was excelling at basketball, however, his parents were splitting up. They didn't come to his games any more. Their own problems took over their lives, and Gary—although he lived with his mother—was on his own. His two younger sisters took up his mom's time, and his dad stopped having contact with the family.

When he was a senior Gary gave up on school and sports. No one encouraged him to excel in anything, so, he thought, why bother?

Gary had friends on the basketball team, but once he stopped practicing with the team they ignored him. They were too wrapped up in their own lives of study and practice to notice that Gary could have used a supportive friend or two. Instead, they were angry with him for deserting the team.

One day Gary ran into a couple of his old friends from junior high. They told him they had dropped out of school and joined a gang. They asked what Gary was up to; "Nothing," he told them. They invited him to hang around with them for a while.

Soon Gary was a member of the gang. He liked the members, and the gang became his surrogate family. They had guns, they sold drugs, and they always had plenty of money and nice clothes; but none of that really mattered to Gary. What mattered to him was that he belonged somewhere. The gang leader, a drug dealer, became his role model.

Why Gary Joined the Gang

Gary didn't really have trouble at home; however, he was suddenly ignored by his mother, and his father was nowhere to be found. He needed to look beyond his family for approval and security. The gang became his extended family.

Unfortunately, Gary's new friends were traveling on a road to nowhere: They were either going to end up in jail or, worse, be injured or even killed in gang warfare.

Gary's gang were involved in the warfare because they wanted to protect "their neighborhood," where members did their drug business. Most of the members were from poor and broken homes. However, Gary's family was not poverty-stricken. His mom worked; there was food on the table. Gary joined the gang out of spite; he wanted attention, and this was one way to get it. Other members joined because they thought it was a way to a better life.

Gary eventually was caught selling drugs; he was convicted and put in prison for five years. There he had plenty of time to reflect on what he had chosen to do with his life.

Gary was disappointed in himself. He wished he had sought the help of an adult he trusted. He was determined to change his life. When he was allowed to go to the prison library, he read books on various vocations and careers. He worked at getting his high school diploma.

Gary decided he would like to become a counselor to help kids like himself stay on track. He knew he had a lot to give others. He knew firsthand that education could lead to a better life whereas gangs and drugs could only lead to prison or death.

Little did he know at the time that programs to prevent young people from joining gangs were starting up all over the country. And the need for counselors for these programs was growing.

Feeling Pressured?

If teens are thinking about or feeling pressured to join a gang, they should look for help from school counselors or other adults they trust. As Gary found out, gang members' lives go nowhere.

Many U.S. cities have programs that are fighting the teenage gang problem; teens can find out what their city is doing through their school counselors or local youth centers.

CHAPTER ◇ 10

Helping Your Parents
Understand

Families in the 1990s can be confusing. Mothers work, fathers work, and for the young person, there are often stepmothers, stepfathers, and stepsiblings to cope with too.

The divorce rate remains at close to 50 percent, which means that 40 to 50 percent of U.S. teens are living in single-parent households. They may be on their own while a parent works to run a household alone.

Depending on the family situation, some parents give teens too much freedom while others give them too much protection.

School counselors say that whatever the situation, teenagers may depend on their friends instead of their parents for understanding. Teens may look to their peers to help them through changes, and parents may not approve of the friends they choose.

Parents must realize, however, that a young person's

choice of clique or friends is a first step in separating from them.

Independence through Friends

Child study experts say that parents may have trouble dealing with the fact that their children are growing up and looking for independence and accepting that the teens are doing so through choosing cliques or friends.

It's a confusing time for both parents and young people, and the more teens can communicate with their parents, the better off everyone will be.

Ginger

Ginger, a sophomore in high school, was an only child. Her parents, well educated and hard workers, both were employed outside of the home. She had been a latchkey kid since she was in the third grade.

There wasn't much conversation during the week while she was growing up, but on the weekends— after all the errands were taken care of—her parents would ask her about school. However, they never seemed to listen to her answers.

They never paid much attention to her choice of friends either; when friends dropped by to pick her up, her parents would smile and say, "Have a nice time."

The summer before her sophomore year her parents split up. She was given the choice of which parent to live with; she chose her mother.

Soon, however, Ginger and her mother began having problems. Suddenly, the mother decided that she should control Ginger's life.

She began taking a closer look at Ginger's friends—her friends since junior high school and mostly latch-key kids like herself. Ginger's mother criticized these young people, saying they had no guidance—which now, of course, Ginger did. She took a hand in Ginger's social life, pushing her to make more "note-worthy" friends. She did not understand that Ginger was happy with the friends she already had.

Ginger and her friends were not overly involved in school activities, but that's the way they wanted it. They spent a lot of time talking to each other—they always had. Their parents were never around, so they had each other to talk to.

Ginger's mother kept pushing Ginger to meet new people. Ginger started staying over at her friends' home later and later, not wanting to deal with her unhappy mother and all her complaints.

Her mother became angry and grounded her. Ginger promptly packed her bag and went to live with her father on the other side of town.

Her mother was furious.

Communication and Trust

Young people can do two things to help parents understand them better:

- Communicate: Let your parents know what's going on in your head.
- Establish trust: Always be honest.

Keep in mind, however, that even if you do your part, your parents may not do theirs.

In other words, parents need to be aware of what's

happening on the local teen scene and in their own home. If they're not, it's up the teens to inform them.

Ginger's situation shows that there was a communication problem between her and her mother that started when Ginger was little. Parents should discuss their expectations for their children's behavior. Ginger's parents had never done that, and when her mother decided to do so, it was so abrupt that Ginger became angry.

Agreements and Rules

School counselors say that parents also may go through a denial stage—they refuse to believe that their kids are growing up.

Then they may try to exert too much control. This may have happened to Ginger's mother. Parents' rules suddenly become stricter, and that can create trouble.

After parents and teens discuss expectations, they should agree on the rules. If both sides keep the agreement, trust will be there and some of the trouble is likely to be alleviated.

If the rules are broken, parents need to enforce the agreed-upon consequences for breaking that trust. But if the trust is broken, parents and child need to reestablish it. Both sides need to be willing to start over.

Complaints from Kids

Jep Enck, who has worked with young people for many years, says that the main complaints teens have about parents/adults are the following. See if you have similar complaints.

1. **Comparisons**
   - "Your brother never did that."
   - "Sally was always more open with me."
   - "You don't seem to care about grades as your sister does."
2. **Put-downs**
   - "You look like a tramp."
   - "Where did you get that weird outfit?"
   - "Your friends are trash."
3. **Failure to listen**
   - They are told their teen's feelings and then tell him or her not to feel that way.
   - They try to change the teen's perception to their own.
   - They lecture.
4. **Adultisms**
   - "I've told you a thousand times . . ."
   - "When I was your age . . ."
   - "If you ever do that again . . ."
   - "Why can't you ever . . ."
5. **Acting pally**
   - They try to act too much like the young person.
   - They tell their kids too much about their own problems.
6. **Overprotectiveness**
   - They don't let the children make mistakes.
   - They don't let the children forget their mistakes.
   - They keep the children too dependent.
7. **Easy to con**
   - They don't see through their children.
   - They agree to everything.
   - They don't stand up for themselves.

8. **Hypocrisy**
   - They don't follow through on threats.
   - They say one thing and do another.
9. **Dogmatism**
   - They won't bend.
   - They have their minds made up.
   - They see things only one way.
10. **Unavailability**
    - They are too busy.
    - They are preoccupied with their own lives and issues.
11. **Seriousness**
    - They have no sense of humor.
    - They take themselves and their children too seriously.
    - They see themselves as inadequate parents.

You may find topics here that you can bring up for discussion with your parents. Start communicating.

Talking, Talking, Talking

Experts agree that teenagers differ in their social needs. Unlike Ginger, some teens need many friends and a busy social schedule to feel happy or complete. Others are content with just a few friends.

If teens are not as social as parents might want them to be, a parent needs to understand that this may be what their children are happy and comfortable with. Teens need to communicate that fact to pushy parents.

And pushing a teen may backfire, as it did in Ginger's case. Parents need to accept and respect their children's choice of friends.

Troublemakers

There will always be teens who for some reason get hooked up with "bad influences." Kids may hang around with cliques that misbehave or break the law.

The best way for parents to intervene is to be good role models themselves.

If teens feel that their parents' behavior is not up to par, is in some way not acceptable, maybe even embarrassing, they should communicate their concerns to their parents.

On the other hand, parents should explain why their children's choices are unacceptable. They need to communicate their concerns and offer suggestions.

Teens must realize that even though they are on their way to gaining independence, their parents still need to be involved in their lives. Even if they have had a good upbringing, teenagers still need guidance.

In other words, parents should approach their children with the attitude, "It's not that I want to be unreasonable, but I am concerned about your welfare."

If parents are concerned about your choice of friends, they should ask you why a particular friend is so important to you. If they don't ask, you need to take the initiative and tell them why this friend is so important.

Perhaps you're hanging around this "bad influence" because you are trying to help him or her become a better person. Parents should not automatically assume that you're being dragged down by the other teen. Maybe you're acting as a role model.

Before you approach your parents for a discussion, counselors suggest that you think through your answers to the following questions:

- Why do your parents think differently than you do? Why do they not like your friend?
- What are the issues? They don't like your friend because he or she smokes or drives a beat-up car? They don't like your friend's parents? What *is* the problem?
- Are there students who have worse problems than you have with your parents? Are you blowing your problems out of proportion?

When you talk to your parents, use "I" statements. For example, "This is why I think this . . . Mom, I am really troubled . . . I feel sad because you don't like my friends." Don't use the accusatory "you" statement.

Usually parents can't influence whom you pick for friends. And a parent's judgment isn't always right. That's why it's so important to communicate and be honest.

When you parents don't like your friends, sit down and talk about it. But remember, talk to them at a good time—not the minute they get home from work or when they want to watch a special show.

And More Talking

If you are having a extraordinarily difficult time talking to your parents, consider speaking with another adult whom you trust.

Is there someone who would understand? Is there someone who could act as a liaison?

Also, invite your friends over to meet your parents, or ask your parents to go to a movie with you and your friends. Try for a mature approach, and help your parents see your friends as you see them.

CHAPTER 11

Siblings and Cousins

Cassie and Erika

Cassie was fourteen, fat, and unhappy. Her seventeen-year-old sister Erika was pretty, a cheerleader, and very popular. Cassie was a freshman, Erika a senior.

Because Erika was pretty and friendly, she had sailed through high school with few problems and plenty of friends. Cassie, however, was scared. In her first year of high school she was feeling very insecure. She had hoped that her sister would bail her out—introduce her to people. But that was not to be. Instead, Erika ignored Cassie.

The sisters' last name was an unusual one—Simborski. Therefore, Cassie was constantly asked by teachers and classmates if Erika was her sister. When she said yes she usually got a reply such as "Really?"

Cassie was being compared to her sister, and she didn't like it—especially since Erika was treating her so badly.

At home, Cassie complained to her parents that Erika wouldn't introduce her to anyone or eat lunch with her.

When her parents asked Erika what the problem was, she said: "These are my friends, they are not Cassie's! I made them on my own, and she can find her own friends—just like I did!"

Case closed.

Often brothers and sisters are very different from each other, as in the case of Cassie and Erika.

Although Cassie was shy, it was up to her to make her own friends in her own way. Erika was right: They were her friends that she made on her own. It was not her responsibility to share them with her sister.

However, the unfortunate thing was that people who knew Erika—teachers and students—compared Cassie to her sister. Two very different people.

That is not fair, but it often happens when younger siblings follow their elders through school. If an older sibling is an A student or an outstanding athlete, the younger sibling may be unfairly compared to him or her.

After Cassie's first semester, she talked with her school counselor and her parents about how she was constantly compared to Erika. She asked to be transferred to one of the other two high schools in town so she could have her own identity. Her request was granted.

Often, however, that solution may not be possible, and siblings just have to grit their teeth, stay where they are, and prove that they are individuals, not clones of their older siblings.

Kyle and Tyler

Kyle Balandran was a troublemaker at school from day one. He got by with fair grades, but ever since grade school he had been the class clown, the guy who disrupted class whenever he could. Consequently, he was always in the principal's office.

Kyle's friends were all troublemakers; he belonged to a clique of clowns and cut-ups. They were famous for their antics, and when they graduated all their teachers gave a sigh of relief.

Enter Tyler Balandran, Kyle's younger brother. The fall after Kyle graduated, Tyler was ready to start high school.

The brothers looked a lot alike, but they were very different. Tyler was serious about school; he wanted to go to college, and his dream was to become a veterinarian. Kyle, however, went to work at a record store after graduation and still had no direction in life.

Tyler, however, received a cold reception from teachers and administrators. In classes where teachers remembered Kyle, they always directed comments about "order in the classroom" toward Tyler and the latest class clowns.

Tyler worked hard during the first two or three weeks of school, yet most teachers still expected him to act up. He felt he had to do something.

He first talked with his friends, but they had no answers.

Next, Tyler went to his parents, who knew how hard he was trying and how serious a student he was. They promised to call the school and talk with a counselor.

The counselor, in turn, talked with each of Tyler's teachers, explaining the problem. Most were understanding, and soon Tyler became a respected and well-liked student.

One older teacher couldn't get past the fact that Tyler was Kyle's brother and continued to pick on him. But when Tyler consistently scored well on quizzes and tests, the teacher changed his attitude. Tyler had only to prove himself.

Although Tyler and his friends were nothing like his brother's, Tyler was put in a false light by his teachers.

The first few weeks of high school were rough, but Tyler was smart enough to realize that he couldn't handle the problem alone. He went to adults he trusted, his parents in this case.

Travis

Travis Hernandez, fourteen, lived in East Los Angeles; he was an only child. Many of his aunt and uncles, who lived in Colorado, had lots of children, however. Thus, he had many cousins.

Travis remembered fondly the last time he had visited Colorado; he was ten and his family stayed for two weeks. He recalled how nice it was to be in a small town where you could walk the streets at night and not be afraid! In fact, from many of his relatives' homes he and his cousins could walk downtown, to parks, for ice cream, or to the movies. He also remembered how much fun he had with all his cousins, seven of whom were around his age.

Now the family was going to Colorado again. Travis couldn't wait! Little did he know what was ahead.

First, Travis was developing very slowly physically; he still looked ten years old.

Second, Travis had become a bookworm. When he

found out about the trip he checked out a lot of books on the history of Colorado and the American West. He also read about Rocky Mountain National Park, which was near where his relatives lived. He hoped that some of his older cousins who could drive would take him there.

Third, in the four years since Travis had seen his cousins, a lot had happened to all of them. Many of them disliked each other and were in separate cliques, and one boy was in a small-time street gang. Nature and reading were not subjects that interested any of his cousins.

When Travis and his family arrived, none of his cousins wanted anything to do with him; in fact, they called him "the shrimp" behind his back.

Travis was hurt, and he found himself spending time with cousins who were much younger than he. He did go to Rocky Mountain National Park, but with his parents and an uncle.

Travis, although hurt by his cousins' behavior, finally accepted his situation with his relatives. When the adults asked why he wasn't going out with his cousins, he would reply that he didn't feel like it, not that they didn't ask him to go.

He realized that he really didn't want to do the things his cousins were doing anyway. They didn't seem to have anything in common any more—values or morals.

People and places don't often stay the same—especially after four years. Travis's vacation was different this time, but he learned a lesson about change and how even cousins can turn into judgmental cliques. Maintaining his self-esteem helped him get through the vacation.

CHAPTER 12

Socializing

Parties, church socials, school organization meetings. All teens want to feel accepted and comfortable at these events. They're good places to meet new friends and have fun.

But such activities are not without their problems . . .

Cary and Judy

Cary and Judy, twin brother and sister, moved to a new town during their junior year. During the first month of school, they had each other. They walked to school together and had lunch together. But then both of them began talking to classmates, and soon they had their own acquaintances at school.

However, they still didn't have much of a social life after school or on weekends.

In October Cary was invited to a Saturday night party by Emily, a girl in his Family Living class; he asked if he could bring Judy, and she said, "But, of course!"

Emily explained that her parents would be there, and no drugs or alcohol would be allowed. Still, Cary and Judy heard that "everybody" would be at the party.

Cary felt confident about going to the party because he was sure that Emily had a crush on him and would take care of him; in other words, she would introduce him to the others and make him feel comfortable.

Judy, on the other hand, was in a panic. She was a bit shy and felt better when she met one person at a time. However, she thought she should go to the party because it was an opportunity to meet more people. Besides, she could hang out around Cary. He would be there if she got in some kind of awkward situation.

How should Cary and Judy prepare for this party? Judy, especially, needs to feel confident and at her best.

Judy is one step ahead of the game because she's going with her brother; she doesn't have to show up alone. Teens who don't have such a convenient situation should consider going with a friend. That way they'll have each other.

Judy begged Cary to ask what kind of party it was to be so she could choose the right kind of clothes. He called Emily and found out that it was definitely not a casual affair. Teens were to dress up a bit.

Judy then was able to choose something appropriate yet comfortable. She knew that if she wore something she felt good in, that was a step in the right direction. In other words, don't wear shoes that hurt your feet or jeans so tight you can't breathe; it will just add to your discomfort.

Judy also had to mentally prepare herself to be left alone eventually by Cary. She knew she would have to circulate and meet people on her own. After all, that's why she was going.

At the party, Emily took Cary with her right away. He shrugged at Judy and disappeared. Then Judy saw a girl she knew from history class but had never met. Taking a deep breath, she went over and introduced herself, asking how she did on the last quiz. That worked fine and soon the girl began introducing Judy to others.

By the end of the evening both Cary and Judy had met many new people; their circle of acquaintances was much wider than when they arrived.

Not all parties end on such a happy note, however.

Dustin and Caitlin

Dustin and Caitlin, both ninth-graders, were invited to a party at Jude's house. They didn't know each other, but they met at the party. They were probably drawn to each other because they both were wearing all black.

In their school district, ninth grade was part of the high school. They admitted to each how really young and stupid they'd felt when school started.

They talked about their host Jude, a junior. They didn't know much about him, but they admired him from afar; he seemed so smart and cool. Caitlin had met Jude in art class, and Dustin had met him on the magazine staff.

When there was a moment of silence in their conversation, Dustin and Caitlin decided that they should mingle. What they discovered wasn't so cool.

In one corner a group of kids were doing shots of tequila, and in another corner joints were being passed. Dustin and Caitlin talked with both groups but soon found that they were just braggarts and were putting down everyone who wasn't at the party.

Dustin and Caitlin were glad they had met, but the rest of Jude's friends turned them off.

Teens should remember that it's always good to mingle with others and find out what they're all about. The more they know about others' life-styles, the better they will be at choosing one of their own.

Consider the following when you are about to socialize with a new clique.

- Do you have anything in common with this group? Do they enjoy doing the things you like?
- Do the members make you feel welcome or good about yourself? Or do you constantly find yourself doing things to gain their acceptance or attention? Can you be yourself?
- Do they do drugs or alcohol or anything else you don't approve of?
- Do they share your values? For example, do they think putting down a particular ethnic group is okay, but you don't?

Many teens today find themselves in social situations where drugs and alcohol are used. And they may not feel comfortable.

All across the country groups of teens are forming groups such as SADD (Students Against Drunk Driving) that promote nonalcoholic and drug-free parties. Such events show adolescents that they can have a good time while staying straight.

If teens' families are members of a church, youth organizations and activities usually abound there. This is a good place to meet new people, but teens should realize that even at church, cliques exist.

Many young people find that doing volunteer work is not only satisfying but also a way to meet new people.

Teenagers should realize that there are many satisfying and fun cliques in their town whose members don't use drugs and alcohol. Those who are in search of a new or different social life have many options.

Following are some suggestions for volunteering and for spending time drug-free and alcohol-free.

Religious Youth Groups.   With religious youth activities, young people usually get together in a spiritual environment, but not always.

Many teen religious groups are connected with churches or synagogues where families worship. Other groups are national and interdenominational, such as the organization called Young Life.

Many teens enjoy being part of a religious group because they find others with the same values.

Church groups may organize dances, camping trips, and discussion groups with topics ranging from the environment to religion. In the national groups, helping others is a big part of activities. For instance, they help senior citizens paint their homes or rebuild their roofs— whatever needs to be done.

Community Service.   For many teens, volunteering has become an important part of their lives. However, young people need to find the volunteer program that is right for them.

For instance, if teenagers have an interest in a particular cause—such as the environment—they'll have more fun helping out with an organization that is involved with saving the planet. And they'll be working with others who share their interests.

When teens know what cause they would like to help with, they can ask the school counselor if there is an organization devoted to that cause. Often communities have a volunteer clearinghouse for programs that need help.

Or teens can telephone such organizations as the Red Cross, United Way, the public library (literacy programs), the Salvation Army, the local homeless shelter, the American Association of Retired Persons (senior citizens), the local hospital, nursing homes, or the area Sierra Club (environment).

Maddie

Sixteen-year-old Maddie started drinking at parties when she was thirteen and in junior high. Alcohol was easy to get; her clique was an older crowd. They'd just go to liquor stores and ask someone to buy whatever they wanted. No problem.

Maddie thought people liked her better after she had a couple of drinks, and she thought she was funnier. She also tried drugs, but mostly she just drank.

But then she started drinking all the time; she started before school and continued throughout the day. By the time she was fifteen she was dependent on alcohol. She needed help, and she got it, but she needed months of therapy. She met other young people with similar problems in a support group she joined.

Now at sixteen Maddie has new friends, many of them from the group; she had to drop her old ones. Her new clique doesn't drink, and all of them have to be creative to come up with new, fun things to do in their spare time.

Drinking had become such a normal activity in Maddie's old group that it was difficult for her to think of other ways to have fun with a group of friends. Maddie knew, however, that she couldn't drink; she had to socialize just being herself.

Following are a few suggestions for group activities:

• When the weather's nice, go on a hike on a Saturday or Sunday and take a picnic along.
• Have a dinner party like adults. Plan a menu and have everyone bring a course. You can add to the fun by asking that everyone dress in their Sunday best for the occasion.
   Or try something out of the 1960s: have a fondue party. Check your parents' cookbooks for a recipe and ask around for a fondue pot—someone's got to have one! You sit around and cook little pieces of meat in hot oil or dip chunks of French bread in melted cheese. This meal takes a long time to eat, so there's plenty of time for conversation.
• Play miniature golf. With a big group, it will take a while to make it around the course—plenty of time for talking and kidding around.
• Try bowling. It's inexpensive, and lots of players

can participate. Split into two teams, and the team that loses buys the refreshments.

- Have a video marathon weekend, with everyone bringing his or her favorite film; then rate which one is the best. Make everyone give a little speech about why this video is the best movie ever made. Have plenty of refreshments on hand.
- Make a huge collage poster. Everyone brings old magazines and scissors. You'll need some large poster board—as big as you can get it—and some rubber cement. Then start cutting and pasting. Soon you'll have a colorful, unique poster. Hold a drawing to see which one of your gang gets to keep it. Make two or three if your group is ambitious.

CHAPTER ◇ 13

Friends in the Work World

Katie

Sixteen-year-old Katie was tired of not having any money. She got an allowance, but it was only $5 a week and sometimes her parents didn't even have that to give her. Her friends all got at least $10 a week, and her best friend, Bitsy, always had cash.

So Katie decided to get a job. She figured she could work somewhere two or three days a week after school and on weekends.

She applied at the nearest mall, which was within walking distance of both her home and her school, for a job at one of the concessions in the food court. She was amazed at how much she might be paid per hour: $4.50 to $4.90. That was almost as much as her weekly allowance!

Katie filled out applications at three fast-food operations; the yogurt stand manager sounded hopeful.

He expected a position to be open in a couple of days.

The job did materialize, and Katie started work. She worked from 4 to 9 p.m. Tuesdays, Thursdays, and Fridays and from noon to 6 p.m. on Saturdays and Sundays. That was 27 hours a week to start.

Katie's parents were upset at the number of hours she had taken, yet they were proud—and somewhat relieved—that she was making her own money.

Katie worked with two other teens, April and Adam, and with the manager or assistant manager. The two managers, Bill and Bob, were both twenty-one.

Katie was nervous at first, but once she knew the prices and how to fix all the sundaes and shakes, the work was a breeze. Sometimes the customers got cranky, but she didn't mind. The only thing she minded was how tired her feet and legs got, and when she got off work she was exhausted.

Because she was so tired, she stopped doing her homework when she got home. In fact, she started hanging around with her coworkers instead.

One Saturday, after Katie had been working for about a month, Bob asked her to go out with him that night. She had plans with Bitsy and her gang to go to the movies. She did miss Bitsy, but going out with an older man seemed exciting.

"Come on," Bob said. "We'll double-date with April and Bill."

That sounded fun, so Katie agreed. Bitsy was not so pleased.

"Oh, so now you're going to hang with your working world friends, huh? Those greasy fast-food types," Bitsy said with anger in her voice.

"Bitsy, please. They are not greasy, and I have a lot of fun working with these people; they are new friends," Katie tried to explain.

"Well," Bitsy said, "okay, but aren't you afraid of going out with an older guy? He might try some stuff, you know?"

"Ah, Bob is a nice guy," Katie said. "I trust him completely."

"Well, give me a call when you can find the time," Bitsy said and hung up.

Through her first job, Katie had quickly made a new circle of friends. And because she was spending so much time at work her old gang quickly began to take second place on her social calendar.

With her friends from work, she could share stories about goofy customers and about funny mistakes they had made during the day. They could also gossip about the folks who worked in the other food stands. Katie's work world became an important part of her life.

Besides, her weekly paycheck after taxes was about $100—more money than she knew what to do with. She decided she would start putting some of it away for college. The only problem was, if she didn't get back to studying her grades might not allow her to attend college!

Katie also was feeling guilty about not seeing her old friends, especially Bitsy; ironically, they were the reason she took the job in the first place. Now she was having a wide range of new experiences, and more kept coming at her.

Katie's Change

On Katie's double-date, Bob and Bill brought along liquor and mixers for everyone. Katie was not much of a drinker; her old gang never experimented much. However, she did have a couple of rum and Cokes that night.

The group didn't do much but drive from park to park looking for parties. When they couldn't find any, Bill and Bob suggested going to their apartment with a pizza and watching "Saturday Night Live." There Katie found herself in an awkward position: Bob tried to force her to have sex with him. She ran from the building and walked three miles home.

Bob was very cold to her the next day at work.

"He is really mad at you," April said. "He thought you were a big girl, if you know what I mean."

"Well, I'm not that kind of girl," Katie said. "I don't put out because someone buys me a pizza."

"Yeah, well, that's good," April said. "But a lot of girls who work in the mall do, and Bob's used to that."

"Well, what am I going to do?" said Katie. "I can't stand working here with all this tension."

"I don't know. Bob won't fire you, but he could make your life miserable. He made the girl you replaced pretty miserable."

Katie did quit. And when she did, she went back to her old clique and discovered how hurt Bitsy really was. Katie opened up to Bitsy and told her about her horrible date and about the uncomfortable atmosphere at work. Because she was honest with Bitsy, the two of them were able to heal the hurts and continue their friendship.

Bitsy said she was interested in working too, but not at the mall. They did some brainstorming. What kind of work could they do together, and maybe just on weekends, so their study habits wouldn't suffer during the week?

The girls came up with a children's party service. They both lived in neighborhoods with seemingly hundreds of grade-school kids and lots of working parents.

They charged the parents a flat fee and took care of all the details, right down to hiring others in the clique to entertain as clowns or cowboys.

Although Katie had a rough experience with her first step into the working world, she learned a lot from it and came out ahead in the end.

Barney

Barney, seventeen, was a waiter at a pizza restaurant. In his senior year in high school, he was working because he needed to. His parents were recently divorced, and he lived with his father. There wasn't much money to go around.

Barney was the senior class treasurer and served on the student council. He was involved in student government because he planned to major in political science in college.

Because he was working about 30 hours a week, he really had no friends at school except for those in student government. Also he had very little time for social life.

Finally, as the Christmas holidays approached, Barney got restless. He was tired of working all the time; he was tired of never having any fun. The pressure got to him, and he found himself partying with his coworkers.

Some of them, although they too were in school, did not care about grades, and they often drank when they got off work at midnight. Often they didn't make it to classes the next morning.

For a couple of weeks Barney drank with four of his coworkers and let his homework go. Then Christmas vacation began, and all he did was work and party.

By the time school had begun again Barney had a routine. Second-quarter grades came out at the end of January, and he slipped to Bs and Cs. Student council and senior class meetings were held before school started, and he was missing them.

Marjorie, the senior class president, was concerned; something was wrong in Barney's life. She knew that his parents were recently divorced, he was working too many hours, and he was missing classes and meetings.

She bumped into him in the hall and asked him to join her for lunch. In the cafeteria, Marjorie got the weary Barney to admit that his life was just too much to handle. He couldn't keep up. He needed a social life, and he admitted that drinking with the guys at the restaurant wasn't what he really wanted—but it was the only social activity that seemed available in his situation.

Marjorie and Barney decided that he needed to talk with his counselor, Mr. Billings.

Mr. Billings first asked Barney if he really needed to work so many hours. Barney admitted that he took more hours than he probably needed because he didn't know how to say no to his manager.

Mr. Billings suggested that if he cut down on his hours he might find time for social activities other than drinking after work. He also might find more time to study and to sleep—so he could start making his morning meetings again.

Barney admitted that his grades and future were more important than a few extra dollars. He admitted that he'd been spending a lot of the extra money on beer, anyway.

Mr. Billings also suggested that he talk to his father. The two hardly ever saw each other because of the hours they kept. He never saw his mother, who lived on the other side of town.

Barney did talk to his father; they discussed the pain they were both feeling because of Barney's mother's absence. They realized that they had both been over-working to avoid that pain. Barney's father was all for his cutting down on work hours; he said he would enjoy having his son around a bit more in the evenings.

Work can be beneficial for teens, but often they do not know how many hours they can handle. They have trouble keeping their priorities straight. Many people, including friends and family, may feel hurt while a teen juggles social life, school, and work.

Teens need to find the correct balance. If they are having trouble coping, they should speak with a school counselor or a parent.

Signs that you're slipping:

- You forget to eat. You might even be losing weight.
- You're missing sleep; you always seem to be tired.
- You can't concentrate in classes.
- You don't make it to class.
- Your grades start slipping.
- You're starting to use drugs and alcohol.

- You don't have time for activities you truly enjoy.
- You're not spending time with your family.
- You don't have time for your friends.
- You start to worry about everything.

Teens can certainly learn and benefit from a part-time job; it can be like a sneak preview of the adult working world. However, teens need to decide whether a paycheck is worth losing friends and high grade point averages. A paycheck can be important, but it shouldn't replace everything else in a teenager's life.

CHAPTER ◇ 14

And After High School?

The transition from high school senior to college freshman or employee in the workforce is a major life change in a young person's life.

Many times it means that a teenager has to leave the family home, move to a new town, and make new friends. Usually, a young person goes from a stage of dependence/ independence to complete independence.

If teens become college students, they may find that university sororities and fraternities can be their "families" away from home and make the transition to independence less scary.

Some students, however, prefer—or must—live in campus dormitories, and dorms and their inhabitants are worlds to themselves.

Many of the suggestions in Chapter 3 on moving can apply to the transition after high school. Teens can use this stage to their benefit.

After high school young people discover that their peer

groups change. They may become involved in a variety of groups and make friends in all of them.

At work, a circle of friends may form. In a dorm, the students who live at the same end of a hall may form a group who do things together. If teens live in an apartment, the same kind of situation can happen, and the ages and interests of friends can vary quite a bit.

As a young person leaves high school, the world of peer groups and peer pressure should begin to dwindle.

All in all, life after high school is a time for making new friends—and a time for becoming independent.

Larry and Lea

Larry and Lea were friends throughout their junior and senior years in high school. They were not romantically involved, only good friends. They were in a clique of kids who used drugs regularly. Neither of them particularly enjoyed doing drugs, but they went along because everyone else did them, and the clique was where they seemed to fit.

Larry and Lea often talked about how they couldn't wait to get to college and start their lives all over. They were both good students, but their grades were lower than they should have been because they so often cut classes with the rest of the clique.

After graduation Lea went to a small private college, where she joined a sorority that did not tolerate drug use. She worked part time in one of the college cafeterias, where she met other students who had to work and were serious about their grades.

Lea missed her family; however, she felt good knowing that she was out on her own—and that

she'd soon get to go home for the one-week Thanks-
giving break.

Because of his family finances, Larry stayed at
home; he worked full time at a restaurant as a
prep cook and attended community college in the
evenings.

Larry was so busy that he made few new friends
except for classmates who were in similar situations.
Yet he was glad to be out of his high school clique,
thinking clearly and working toward a goal.

He was learning to be a responsible student and
juggle the responsibilities of work and school. When
old friends who were still in town called, Larry was
easily "too busy" to go out and get high with them.

The Five Tasks

According to Maureen Conway, director of the Colorado
State University Center for Alcohol Education, five tasks
must be dealt with by young people during the post-high
school transition and beyond:

- Separation from friends or family or both
- Development of an adult identity
- Discovery of who they are sexually
- Discovery of adult relationships with others
- Discovery of a career path

It's a whole new life after high school. By having a
good self-image and using communication skills a teen
should be able to make friendships of the quality—and
quantity—that he or she wishes.

Cliques will never disappear—not after high school,
not after college. They have been around since the

beginning of time, and as you move into adulthood you'll probably be involved in a variety of cliques.

As you get older, you may find that there are many more cliques to choose from; they may be more refined. Just think of all the different kinds of magazines there are: That means that people have hundreds of interests, and each one of those interests represents a potential clique.

Keep using your "visitor's pass" to explore new groups and meet new people throughout your years after high school.

CHAPTER 15

If You Need Outside Help

Kevin

When sixteen-year-old Kevin got his first job—at a large high-tech toy store—he was thrilled. He enjoyed his coworkers, who were young people in their late teens, and he enjoyed the customers, who were mostly brainy kids with lots of questions about the store's products. He worked a couple of days a week after school and every Saturday.

Kevin soon became friends with two of his fellow employees, seventeen-year-old Alicia and nineteen-year-old Cody.

Alicia and Cody liked alternative music, and they played a lot of their favorite tunes for Kevin when they went to each other's homes after work. Then Alicia and Cody began inviting Kevin to attend concerts with them. The three of them would weave their way through the crowds to the front of the auditorium and dance in front of the band together.

Kevin began to like Alicia as more than a friend. But he knew that she and Cody were more than friends too. One day he asked Alicia to meet him after school for a talk.

Over Cokes, they talked about music for a while and about work at the store. Then Kevin got up the nerve to tell Alicia how he felt about her.

To his surprise, she said some positive things back. They held hands across the table while they talked. Then they walked to a nearby park and kissed before parting and going home.

Alicia continued to be Cody's girlfriend, but she and Kevin saw each other behind Cody's back. They went for drives in the nearby mountains in her Volkswagen bug, and they discovered how similar their dreams and goals were.

One day, after Kevin and Alicia had been seeing each other for about two months, Alicia came to work late, looking as if she had been crying. Cody went to her first, asking her what was wrong. She shook him off, asking him to leave her alone for a while. When Kevin approached her, she yelled, "I need time to myself, you two!" The boys shrugged, and the three of them worked in silence for the rest of the afternoon.

After work, Kevin went home and called Alicia. She said she couldn't talk to him then but that they should skip school the next day and meet at their special place for breakfast. Kevin agreed.

The next morning, Alicia was waiting. She looked as if she hadn't slept all night. When Kevin sat down across from her in the booth, she grabbed his hands and held them tight.

After they had ordered, Alicia spoke softly, with tears in her eyes.

"Kevin, I don't know how to tell you this, but Cody and I are going to get married."

"What?" shouted Kevin. "Married? Why do you want to get married? I know your dreams and your goals—you don't want to get married for a long time. There are too many things you want to do!"

"Kevin, Kevin, please, calm down," Alicia pleaded. "You're right. I'm not ready to get married. But yesterday I found out that I'm going to have a baby, Cody's. Last night we decided to get married."

Kevin was silent. A baby. The girl he loved was having someone else's baby and getting married. He couldn't speak. Inside, Kevin felt a deep loss and a deep anger. He knew Alicia cared for him. He knew she wasn't ready for a baby.

"Alicia," he said. "Why do you have to have this baby? Why don't you have an abortion . . . or if you can't do that, why don't you just put the baby up for adoption after you have it? Then you can go on with your life."

"No!" Alicia whispered. "I won't give my baby up. My mom had me when she was 18, and we've been doing fine on our own. She and I have done fine! What if she had given me away when I was born? Huh? What do you think about that?"

Kevin got up and left. He stayed in his room for the rest of the day. The next day he told his parents he had the flu. He skipped school and called in sick at the store.

The next week he skipped school entirely. He quit his job. When the school eventually called his parents and told them Kevin was not attending classes, they decided that his behavior had taken some kind of strange turn and that he needed outside help. They made an appointment with a therapist.

What kind of teen needs outside help, the kind of help that family and friends can't give?

Kevin obviously did. He believed that his closest friends had betrayed him, and he couldn't deal with the hurt and anger.

And Kevin displayed one of the behaviors that specialists say need outside attention: withdrawal from family and friends.

Other symptoms or behaviors that may signal a need for help follow:

- Regular drug or alcohol use.
- Membership in a peer group that is known to use or sell drugs or alcohol.
- Membership in a peer group that is known to be involved in other criminal activities.
- Behavior change; for instance, skipping classes or losing interest in favorite activities.
- Suicidal thoughts or feelings of worthlessness; comments such as: "I'd be better off dead." "The world would be a better place without me."

Kevin was lucky; his parents got help for him.

Other parents, however, may not be so observant. When young people are in that situation, they need to have the courage to seek help on their own.

Says Mary Ann Clemons, a psychiatric nurse, "Of course, it's ideal if they can talk to their parents about their problems. But if not, there are a lot of people out there that want to help them—teachers, counselors. They should seek out someone they trust.

"They'll be really scared at first, and I know how scary it is to make that call, but it's the most important step that anyone can take."

The adult whom the teen chooses to confide in will direct him or her to some qualified counseling service. There an initial evaluation is made, and the seriousness of the problem is decided.

Says Clemons: "Teens should realize that most people who are counselors have become counselors because they have had problems of their own, so they are a lot more understanding than a teen would think.

"It's like talking to a friend, only better, because friends don't have the knowledge to know what to do about the problem."

After the initial evaluation, methods of treatment are considered. That is why it is so important to be honest with the counselor.

There are two choices: inpatient or outpatient treatment.

With inpatient treatment, an adolescent lives at a center where he or she attends classes to keep up with regular schoolwork but also participates in discussion groups. These groups often are made up of teens with similar problems.

Tara

When Tara was eleven her parents sent her to a summer camp for older girls in the Northwest wilderness where she met girls from all over the country.

Tara was always being sent away to some camp or another during the summer; her busy parents had very little time for her.

At the camp Tara shared a cabin with two fourteen-year-olds and two twelve-year-olds.

One night the five smoked cigarettes smuggled into camp by one of them. Tara didn't feel guilty about it; rather, she felt adventurous.

A couple of nights later the "smuggler" asked her cabinmates if they would like to smoke some pot. Not wanting to be an outsider, Tara said yes. For the last week of camp, the girls shared a joint every night before going to bed.

Tara liked the feeling that pot gave her. At home, she asked her sixteen-year-old brother if he could get some for her.

At first Jed was furious. But Tara told him her birthday was coming up, and she only wanted to celebrate.

Finally Jed agreed. He introduced Tara to a dealer, Tommy, who went to his high school. Through Tommy, she was introduced to many other drugs, and she also met many new "friends."

Tara felt popular and cool for the first time in her life; unfortunately, her grades slipped and what little relationship she had with her parents deteriorated to nothing. When she did speak to her parents, it was only to ask for more money—her allowance had run out.

At fourteen Tara was using more expensive drugs, such as cocaine. She needed more money than her parents would ever give her, so she pawned her mother's jewelry. Then, as she bought cocaine from a well-known dealer, she was arrested.

Her parents, not knowing what else to do, grounded her. Tara became very angry and tore up her room. Frightened, her parents decided she needed help.

Placed in a treatment center, Tara remained angry for a long time. She sat through group meetings with kids with similar problems, refusing to talk.

Finally, though, the anger faded and Tara actually began to listen to what the other teens were saying. She heard their problems and understood how similar they were to her own. She was no longer alone.

Whether teens are in outpatient or inpatient treatment, counselors often suggest that they meet with other young people who have similar problems. Often young people can tell each other what they see or hear from them, and that may be better than hearing it from an authority figure.

Sometimes a young person has a secret he or she is hiding, afraid to tell anyone about it. But eventually, as he or she becomes more comfortable with the group and trusts them, that secret may be shared. And once it is out, others may reveal that they have been in similar situations.

In a therapy situation, if a teen has been warned never to tell anybody about an abusive situation at home, a counselor can act to keep the teen safe.

In case of severe depression, a psychiatrist may prescribe one of the many antidepressants available. Depression has a chemical component, and sometimes drugs are prescribed to counteract an imbalance.

Once teens have had therapy, they learn the symptoms and behaviors to look for when they find themselves falling back into old patterns. They should not have to let things get so bad again.

Sometimes an entire family may need help. For instance, Tara's secret finally came out in a group session:

She wanted her parents to pay attention to her; they never had. Tara wanted a family, not drugs. Tara's psychiatrist arranged for the family to get help together.

Says Clemons: "Parents need to understand, too, that teens need to deal with their problems and emotions when they are happening, because if a teen doesn't deal with the problems, it could be detrimental to future relationships.

"You bring all your baggage with you through life . . . if you close the doors on the problems, they will still be there."

As the organization Alcoholics Anonymous puts it: You're only as sick as the secrets you keep.

CHAPTER 16

Hotlines and Other Sources of Assistance

Derek and Christine

Christine was worried about her friend Derek. Juniors in high school, they had been friends since seventh grade.

Recently Derek had gotten in with a clique of kids who did a lot of cocaine. Christine, who was involved in gymnastics, still saw Derek occasionally, but their relationship was no longer close. They used to be able to chat over a milk shake or soft drink; they didn't have to have liquor or do drugs to have fun. However, Derek's older brother home from college had turned him on to cocaine.

Derek became restless and jumpy when he was with Christine. He often snapped at her and had no patience.

Christine wanted to tell Derek's mother something was wrong, but she didn't know whether that was the right thing to do.

Now Derek was beginning to pawn his possessions for drugs. Christine was afraid he'd begin stealing— or dealing—to support his coke habit.

It was time to do something, but what?

If you're worried about yourself, friends, or family members, below are some suggestions of whom to call for help.

If the situation is not an emergency and you know an adult whom you trust, such as a parent, a clergyperson, or a school counselor, you might approach that adult for help.

In an emergency or dangerous situation, however, you should call the police; the emergency number is 911 in most places.

Most communities maintain crisis hotlines. Such hotlines can help you with all kinds of problems, from thoughts of suicide to coping with abusive parents.

Check the emergency section of the phone book. If no crisis hotline is listed there, the local United Way office can usually put you in touch with the right agency.

Christine called the Cocaine Hotline, below, and was put in touch with a center that was able to guide her in a decision about Derek.

Remember that with hotlines you can remain anonymous and they ensure confidentiality.

An "800" prefix means there is no charge for calls. All toll-free 800 numbers can be found by calling 1-800-555-1212.

Teens should remember that plenty of help is available,

and they never need to feel alone. Help is only a phone call away.

NATIONAL NUMBERS

AIDS Hotline: (800) 342-AIDS

Confidential information and referrals provided. Young people also may call the National Teens AIDS Hotline in the early evenings; other kids will answer AIDS questions: (800) 234-TEEN.

Alcoholics Anonymous: (212) 870-3400.

Teens can find the local chapter in the phone book. This is the biggest organization in the country that helps recovering alcoholics.

A teen who has a recovering friend or parent can call (212) 302-7240 for the location of the nearest Al-Anon or Alateen support group.

Big Brothers, Big Sisters of America: (215) 567-7000.

This organization oversees several groups throughout the country; it helps single parents find role models for their children. Check the phone book for an organization near you, or use the number above to find the agency nearest you.

Child Abuse Hotline: (800) 422-4453.

A call to this hotline will enable teens to find out where they can get help in their region.

Cocaine Helpline: (800) COCAINE.

A call to this number can locate help, from treatment programs to family counseling centers.

Just Say No Foundation: (800) 258-2766.

For information on starting a Just Say No club or to find out how to help those who are abusing drugs, teens can call this foundation.

National Council on Alcoholism: (800) NCA-CALL.

Referrals for teenagers who have drinking problems.

National Institute on Drug Abuse: (800) 662-HELP.

Teens can call this number with any kind of question on drug use or problems. NIDA can refer them to agencies in their area. It can also send information on how to help a friend or family member who uses drugs.

National Federation of Parents for Drug-Free Youth (314) 845-7955.

Teens are referred to treatment centers in their area. The hotline also provides videos and pamphlets about drug abuse.

Teen Line: (800) 743-1672.

This hotline manned by teens answers questions about all kinds of problems: relationships, suicide, depression, eating disorders, pregnancy, and drugs and alcohol.

For Further Reading

Sometimes reading about situations that other young people have to deal with—whether real or fictional—may help you work through your own problems.

Many of the following novels encourage you to expand your values and to question the norms. They are categorized by chapters of this book, although they may fit under more than one.

Chapter 1

Callan, Jamie. *Over the Hill at Fourteen.* NAL/Signet/Vista, paperback. A teen model feels insecure.

Colman, Hila. *The Double Life of Angela Jones.* Morrow, 1988. A poor girl from New York receives a scholarship to a private school in New England. She has to decide whether or not to tell the truth about her background.

Greenberg, Jan. *The Pig-Out Blues.* Farrar, Straus & Giroux, 1982. A teen has a weight problem.

Greene, Constance C. *A Girl Called Al.* Dell, 1977. An overweight seventh-grader feels rejected after her parents' divorce.

Hannam, Charles. *A Boy in That Situation: An Autobiography.* Harper & Row, 1977. A young boy suffers insults because he is Jewish and overweight.

Morgenroth, Barbara. *Will the Real Renie Lake Please Stand Up?* Atheneum, 1981. A teen who hangs around with a bad crowd tries to change.

Snyder, Anne. *My Name Is Davy: I'm an Alcoholic.* New American Library, 1978. A high school student starts drinking because he is lonely.

Trivers, James. *I Can Stop Anytime I Want.* Prentice-Hall, 1974. A high school senior starts depending on drugs.

Chapter 2

Bernstein, Jane. *Seven Minutes in Heaven.* Fawcett/Juniper, 1986. Three teen friends go through several crises together.

Kennedy, M. L. *Junior High Jitters.* Scholastic, 1986. A junior high girl is afraid a new girl will take her best friend away.

Knudsen, James. *Just Friends.* Avon/Flare, 1982. Can two boys and one girl remain friends as they all go through changes?

Sachs, Marilyn. *Class Pictures.* E. P. Dutton, 1980. The story of two girls' friendship from kindergarten through 12th grade, focusing on problems in their teen years.

Chapter 3

Carter, Alden. *Growing Season.* Putnam, 1984. A high school senior moves from the city to the country.

Gerber, Merill Joan. *Please Don't Kiss Me Now.* Dial, 1981. A teen struggles with change: a divorce, a friend's death, and a possible move.

Petersen, P.J. *Would You Settle for Improbable?* Delacorte Press, 1981. A boy enters ninth grade after attending a reform school.

Rodowsky, Colby F. H. *My Name is Henley.* Farrar, Straus & Giroux. After moving with her mother from place to place, a teen finds a place she refuses to leave.

Chapter 4

Arrick, Fran. *Chernowitz!* Bradbury Press, 1981. A teen is picked on because he is Jewish.

Bunn, Scott. *Just Hold On.* Delacorte, 1982. Two seniors support each other through the school year.

Elfman, Blossom. *The Return of the Whistler.* Houghton Mifflin, 1981. A boy realizes that his rich friends' values are not his.

Marzollo, Jean. *Do You Love Me, Harvey Burns?* Dial Books, 1983. Anti-Semitism appears when Lisa dates a Jewish teen.

Scoppetone, Sandra. *Long Time Between Kisses.* Harpers, 1982. A nonconformist girl deals with her peers.

Chapter 5

Angier, Bradford, and Cocoran, Barbara. *Ask for Love and They Give You Rice Pudding.* Houghton Mifflin, 1977. A rich teen discovers that money can't buy him friends.

Conrad, Pam. *Taking the Ferry Home.* Harper, 1988. Two very different teens become very good friends.

Makris, Kathryn. *A Different Way.* Avon, 1989. A new girl at high school wonders if being with the "in" crowd is really what she wants.

O'Donnell, Jan. *A Funny Girl Like Me.* Scholastic/Wildfire, 1980. A girl thinks she will be popular if she acts goofy.

Chapter 6

Brancato, Robin F. *Blinded by the Light.* Knopf, 1978. A girl tries to rescue her brother from a religious cult.

Gilmour, H.R. *Ask Me If I Care.* Fawcett/Juniper, 1985. A girl dates a drug pusher and becomes a drug user herself.

Peck, Richard. *Princess Ashley.* Delacorte, 1987. A teenage girl questions the price of friendship when she is put in an awkward position.

Chapter 7

Anaya, Rudolfo. *Bless Me, Ultima.* Quinto Sol Books, 1976. A Mexican family's customs and beliefs are the background for this story about a young boy growing up in New Mexico.

Bentancourt, Jeanne. *More Than Meets the Eye.* Bantam, 1990. A white girl's friendship with a Chinese-American boy brings out prejudice among her "friends."

Blair, Cynthia. *Crazy in Love.* Ballantine, 1988. A Jewish girl is in love with a Puerto Rican boy.

Dorris, Michael. *A Yellow Raft in Blue Water.* H. Holt, 1987. American Indian women of today tell their stories.

Haley, Alex. *Roots.* Dell, 1977. A true story. The author looks for his roots and finds himself in a tiny village in West Africa.

Irwin, Hadley. *Kimi/Kimi.* Macmillan, 1987. Brought up in an all-white town, a Japanese-American teen searches for her Oriental roots.

Santiago, Danny. *Famous All Over Town.* New American Library, 1983. The story of a 14-year-old Chicano boy who lives in East Los Angeles.

Chapter 8

Wersba, Barbara. *Tunes for a Small Harmonica.* Harper & Row, 1976. A noncomformist teen learns to cope.

Chapter 9

Ashley, Bernard. *Terry on the Fence.* Phillips, 1977. A young teen joins a gang.

Childress, Alice. *A Hero Ain't Nothing But a Sandwich*. Avon, 1973. Drugs and peer rejection in Harlem.

Myers, Walter Dean. *Scorpions*. Harper, 1988. Set in Harlem, gang warfare is the focus of this book.

Chapter 10

Carkeet, David. *The Silent Treatment*. Harper, 1988. A teen makes friends with someone his parents don't approve of.

Colman, Hila. *Sometimes I Don't Love My Mother*. Morrow, 1977. The story of a stressful mother-daughter relationship.

Corcoran, Barbara. *Hey, That's My Soul You're Stomping On*. Atheneum, 1978. By looking at her friends' relationships with their mothers, a teen learns about her own.

Reed, Kit. *The Ballad of T. Rantula*. Little Brown, 1979. A boy seeks comfort from his friends when his parents split up.

Van Leeuwan, Jean. *Seems Like This Road Goes On Forever*. Dial, 1979. A girl's overbearing parents cause her to start shoplifting.

Chapter 11

MacLeod, Charlotte. *Maid of Honor*. Atheneum, 1984. A girl's family is wrapped up in her sister's wedding and pays no attention to her.

Miller, Sandy. *Freddie the Thirteenth*. New American Library, 1985. From a family of sixteen, Freddie hides the fact from a boy she likes.

Wells, Rosemary. *None of the Above*. Dial, 1974. After a teen's father remarries, she finds herself dealing with parental pressure and sibling rivalry.

Chapter 12

Butterworth, William Edmund. *Under the Influence*. Four Winds, 1979. A teen's drinking leads to tragedy.

Roos, Stephen. *You'll Miss Me When I'm Gone*. Doubleday, 1988. A teen in a private school tries to hide a drinking problem.

Chapter 13

Asher, Sandy. *Everything Is Not Enough*. Delacorte, 1987. A teen's life changes when he takes a job as a busboy at a restaurant.

Bentancourt, Jeanne. *Not Just Party Girls*. Bantam, 1989. Three teens run a children's party service.

Zindel, Paul. *I Never Loved Your Mind*. Harper, 1970. Two dropouts work in a hospital.

Chapter 14

Butterworth, W.E. *Flunking Out*. Four Winds Press, 1981. Two teens in college find friendship.

Greene, Bette. *Them That Glitter and Them That Don't*. Knopf, 1983. A student thinks her only way out of a small town in Arkansas is through her musical talent.

Hentoff, Nat. *Jazz Country*. Harper, 1965. A graduating senior has to decide between going to college and pursuing a career in jazz music.

Myers, Walter Dean. *Hoops*. Delacorte, 1981. A teen hopes that his basketball skills will help him get out of Harlem.

Springstubb, Tricia. *The Moon on a String*. Little Brown, 1982. A young woman leaves her small town for a job in Boston.

Chapter 15

Dorman, N.B. *Laughter in the Background*. Elsevier/Nelson Books, 1980. A girl asks her school principal for help with her mother's alcoholism.

Howard, Ellen. *Gillyflower*. Atheneum, 1986. A girl who is sexually abused by her father finally tells an adult.

Meyer, Carolyn. *Elliott and Win.* Atheneum, 1986. A boy's mother signs him up with a group that matches adult males with fatherless boys.

Sweeney, Joyce. *Right Behind the Rain.* Delacorte, 1987. A junior in high school discovers that her older brother wants to commit suicide.

Nonfiction

Bauman, Lawrence. *The Nine Most Troublesome Teenage Problems.* Secaucus, NJ: Lyle Stuart Inc., 1986.

Bing, Leon. *Do or Die.* New York: Harper Collins Publishers, 1991.

Booher, Dianna Daniels. *Help! We're Moving.* New York: Julian Messner, 1983.

Johnson, Eric W. *How to Live Through Junior High School.* Philadelphia: J.P. Lippincott Company, 1959.

Kaplan, Leslie S. *Coping with Peer Pressure.* New York: The Rosen Publishing Group, 1990.

Keyes, Ralph. *Is There Life After High School?* Boston: Little, Brown and Company, 1976.

Mayer, Barbara. *The High School Survival Guide.* Lincolnwood, IL: VGM Career Horizons—National Textbook Company, 1986.

McCoy, Kathy. *Changing and Choices: A Junior High Survival Guide.* New York: Perigee Books—Putnam Publishing Group, 1989.

Powledge, Fred. *You'll Survive!* New York: Charles Scribner's Sons, 1986.

Wirths, Claudine G., and Bowman-Kruhm, Mary. *I Hate School: How to Hang In and When to Drop Out.* New York: Thomas Y. Crowell, 1987.

Index